THE
OUTSIDE
WORLD

THE
OUTSIDE
WORLD

BARRY DEMPSTER

PEDLAR PRESS | ST JOHN'S

ACKNOWLEDGEMENTS
The publisher wishes to thank the Canada Council for the Arts and the NL Publishers Assistance Program for their generous support of our publishing program.

LIBRARY AND ARCHIVES CANADA
CATALOGUING IN PUBLICATION

Dempster, Barry, 1952-, author
    The outside world / Barry Dempster.

ISBN 978-1-897141-59-5 (PBK.)

    I. Title.

PS8557.E4827098 2013   C813'.54   C2013-906021-9

EDITORIAL SUPPORT Alayna Munce

COVER ART Micheal Zarowsky, *Lido Bikes No. 31*

DESIGN Zab Design & Typography, Toronto

TYPEFACE Plantin

PRINTED IN CANADA

For Karen

ONE

MY MOTHER'S VIEW wasn't interesting, just a skinny street in Scarborough called Arizona Avenue. Our crabapple tree was laden with wormy apples in summer, snow and ice in winter, pink blossoms in spring. From the window the four houses across the street appeared to be sitting in the crabapple's branches, like extensions of one giant tree house.

This is what I remember: Mom kneeling backwards on a small orange-velour chair, peeking out from behind the curtains. She's been doing this, morning, noon and night. She has forgotten about the existence of the neighbours on either side of us—old lady Allenby and Mr. Rolph, a middle-aged bachelor—she doesn't leave our house, and therefore they don't exist.

I devised a planetary code for Arizona Avenue. The house right across from us, Mrs. Remington's, a Jehovah's Witness, a divorcee with a boyfriend (two definite no-nos in 1966), was Mars. According to Grammie Gorman, she was "scandalous" on all counts. Her daughters Franny and Lucy Remington, identical twins, were a year older than me and amazingly mature, their self-confidence provoking in me a mixture of arousal and repulsion.

Since Jupiter is the largest planet, I assigned it to the Burrs. "A Mr. and a Mrs.," sighed Grammie, her recipe for a perfect family. Mr. Burr was a cop, tall, vaguely threatening. Except for an occasional asthma attack, the Mrs. was unexceptional. Louie Burr was one of my friends so I'm not being mean when I say he was nothing special either. Same with Louie's sister: ordinary as toast. Why Mom enjoyed watching them was beyond me. Only the Burrs' dog, Barfy, with his willingness to stick his nose in anything, occasionally piqued my interest.

If the Burrs were typical, the Costellos were the flip side. Their house was the planet Saturn, a hazy ball half-hidden behind dozens of smoky rings. Both Mr. and Mrs. Costello were chain-smoking alcoholics and their garbage can was always full of empty whisky bottles. Their daughter, Diana, a full-fledged adult of twenty-one, rarely went anywhere other than her own front yard. Weather permitting, she sat on a green canvas garden chair, reading Harlequin romances.

I didn't know much about Uranus, except for the cheap joke it always prompted no matter how old anyone got. Still, someone had to be Uranus. I assigned it to Mr. Milford and his seventeen-year-old son, Lonny, because Lonny was a total asshole: greasy hair to his shoulders, a permanent smirk, and tight jeans with the name MICK scrawled down one leg, JAGGER up the other. Whenever we'd encounter one another, Lonny would give me a look like he was wondering where to bury my body once he'd stabbed me to death.

Mom spent her free time kneeling on the chair, pulling aside both drapes and sheers, and for what? Mrs. Remington, in a pair of red high-heel boots; Barfy, with one leg lifted; Mr. Costello, with a bottle of beer in one hand, a cigarette in the other; Lonny Milford, scratching the J near his crotch. I often wondered what would happen when I grew up. Would I become invisible to her, the world a place where she'd inevitably lose me? She promised she would always keep an eye on my sixteen-year-old mentally retarded sister, Lissy. Knowing she was watching Lissy gave me a fragile sense of safety, but in my teen years I realized that all it would take for me to run away from home would be to turn the corner of our street.

One night we spent an hour at the window, waiting for Dad to wheel into the driveway after one of his twelve-hour days at the Texaco station he ran up on Kingston Road. Mr. Milford and Lonny were tinkering with their old white Chevy, gloves tossed aside on the brown winter grass, their loose scarves dangling above the car's engine. Mr. Burr was halfway up a ladder, putting up Christmas lights, while Louie and his sister were letting Barfy knock them down over and over again. Mr. Costello was sitting on his front porch smoking and drinking. Mrs. Remington's boyfriend was putting the finishing touches on what would be a front lawn skating rink when the days got a little colder. Franny and Lucy were perched on the edge of their porch, two pairs of white figure skates at their feet. Watching the street made me think thin, papery thoughts about Mom, who was so engrossed by the various activities, she hardly registered my presence. No matter what she said about the value of sitting still and taking it all in, being an observer was practically the same thing as being left out. But before I could collapse into a totally dismal mood, snow came rushing out of the clouds, a sudden meteor storm of a blizzard. The snowflakes seemed to be leaving faint skid marks in the air.

Mr. Milford, Lonny and the old white Chevy blended together into a blur. Mr. Burr's ladder might as well have led straight up to outer space, him and the unlit Christmas lights totally swallowed by the whiteout. Same with Franny and Lucy's figure skates, with Mrs. Remington's boyfriend. One look at the Costello porch and it was unclear whether Mr. Costello had gone inside or was buried alive. The only one to outdo the snow was Barfy, who moved faster than the flakes. When Dad came blasting into the scene, our black Valiant looked like the engine of a coal-black train. I closed my eyes and imagined him driving right through our living room window. It was the first time I was conscious of wishing that Dad could be more than he was, the first time I knew that something— something I couldn't even name yet—was going to be smashed.

★

Christmas flew by. Before I knew it, I was back to grade eight, as if the holidays had never happened. I jumped over dozens of tossed-out Christmas trees on my way to school, bits of tinsel still hanging from the needles. Being outside was better than being stuck at home with my mother, but Miss Luther's overheated class, with its scads of maps and charts, its blackboards on two walls completely covered with her miniscule, headache-causing cursive, was another kind of trap—I dragged my dread around that first day like a dead thing on a leash.

By mid-January Miss Luther allowed me independent study, which basically meant that I was handed a topic and told to do anything I wanted with it. The only other student who earned that privilege was Wendy Fergie, a shy girl who kept an eye on everything I did. My latest project was to think about the new Canadian election and compare it with the same process going on in India, where Indira Gandhi's career was about to be launched. I'd rather have tackled the Vietnam War, but when I petitioned Miss Luther, she squeezed her eyes shut and said, "That's too much of a mess, even for you."

I already knew the Canadian election was totally boring. India was much more enticing, brighter, bolder and more crowded than a hundred Scarboroughs. People lived on the streets there, children peed and also washed in the rivers, a man might pull a cart full of passengers as if he were a horse. Who knew what would have happened to my mother if she'd stared out on scenery like that all day. Grade eight India was even more mysterious than my father's grease pit, that hole in the ground where he spent most of his time fixing carburetors and replacing brake shoes, a hot darkness full of guts and wires.

Mom loved to hear stories about my friends' houses: my best friend Marco Morelli and his plastic-wrapped living room sofa, for example, or Louie Burr's bedside rug that had enough dog hair matted into it to make another Barfy. "I knew it, I knew it," she'd say whenever I'd list the sordid details for the umpteenth time. I wondered if my parents knew about the terrible things that went on in other countries. Dad never arrived home in time for the six o'clock news, and by eleven he was usually fast asleep. Mom rarely watched TV, except for two soap operas each day, *The Edge of Night* and *The Secret Storm*, and she never touched the Saturday papers, hating the way their ink turned her fingertips black. How easy for a bungalow and a Texaco station to become the entire world.

*

Sometimes I'd visit the Texaco after school. My friend Marco liked to tag along. He was crazy about the sounds of the ringing cash register and the hoist's metal groans. Me, I preferred the hissing and clicking of the air pump and the glassy clunk when someone bought a bottle of pop from the Coca Cola machine. Dad was too busy to do much more than acknowledge us with a wink or a slap on the shoulder, and we were left alone to explore the greasy supply room or study the road maps or bug Neil, Dad's assistant, a trainee mechanic with slick black hair that he combed into a peak.

This particular day, Dad was hunched over his desk, studying a pile of invoices. Neil was tinkering inside the engine of a brown Pontiac. We busied ourselves putting pennies in the peanut machine, sharing handfuls of salty nuts. It wasn't long before Dad began to talk.

"When I was your age," he began, barely lifting his head from the papers in front of him, "I was working in a butcher shop, ten, sometimes twelve hours a day. Trimming fat and making deliveries. I used to ride my bike through snow up to my waist."

"Wow! Did you ever fall off?"

"I've spent most of my life falling off. I fell off a truck once when I was working for Coca Cola, broke three ribs—pop, pop, pop." He thumped the desk lightly with every pop. "Then I fell off a hydro pole when I was with the City, snapped my left arm in two. Now I fall around here every day. There's so much grease, it's a wonder I haven't cracked my skull."

Marco laughed along with him, but the image of my father

11

cracking his skull made me queasy. I was ready to change the subject, when Dad suddenly swept his right hand across the crowded desk, sending pens and pages and rulers clattering to the floor. There was no anger in the act, just a strangely calm clearing of space.

Marco froze. A yellow invoice came to rest on one of his boots. A green ballpoint hit me on the shin, and then rolled under the bubble gum machine. There were papers everywhere. Was this supposed to be funny, like some of the stuff that happened on *I Love Lucy*? I couldn't tell. Dad stared right through us.

"And they all fell down," he said, shaking his head. "Better get to work, boys. There's a lot of picking up to be done."

When the gas pump bell dinged, Dad stepped over me. An armful of invoices wasn't exactly heavy, but the pages were difficult to stack evenly. The wind from the opening and closing of the front door sent a few papers sailing away. Ten minutes later, his desk re-piled, Dad was now too busy for stories. Cars had lined up at the pumps and an elderly man was waiting in the office to ask about a faulty starter. I didn't bother offering to pitch in, knowing my Dad's line off by heart. *Men's work.*

"Your dad's a great guy," Marco said as we trudged home through the dusk. "My dad doesn't even talk, let alone do crazy things."

I stuck my foot out in front of Marco and tripped him, and he fell into a cruddy mound of snow. The word crazy didn't feel so loaded anymore. On the verge of rage, Marco looked up at me. I narrowed my eyes into slits, like James Cagney in one of his gangster films, and laughed. The reason that Marco was my best friend had a lot to do with his ability to forgive. He preferred being happy and could snap himself out of a bad mood like someone waking up from a hypnotist's trance. I held out my hand. He pulled me down into the snow with him, and the two of us laughed so hard we were snorting.

★

Our house ticked softly, as if the clock were counting down the minutes until time disappeared. A steam iron hissed over a peach-coloured pillow slip. *The Secret Storm* story unfolded on the rec room TV in sudden swells of melodramatic music. Everything was in its place, me curled up in the worn leather armchair, Lissy lying on the rug half-buried beneath her collection of stuffed animals. Mom had decorated the rec room to resemble the cabin of a ship, complete with a Great Lakes steamer's steering wheel, weathered wood and a green captain's lamp. Whenever more playful commercial music came on, Lissy rubbed her fingers together like cricket's wings and made a light chirping sound at the top of her throat.

I was as used to Lissy as I was to the scratched arms of the chair, to the squeaky legs of the ironing board, to the chug-chug-chug of the oil furnace. I hardly noticed how she constantly drooled, or the way she flung herself at things. I never thought about her unless she was right under my nose. I knew some people were afraid of her because she screamed sometimes for no reason, and she'd often hurl herself into anyone's arms, to snuggle up against their chest and wrap her long monkey arms around them. She grunted when she was hungry and spoke in a language that didn't contain a single recognizable word. But fear of Lissy struck me as juvenile; to indulge in it you'd have to be the kind of person who was afraid of shadows and noisy floorboards. Lissy was less harmful than a chair or a radio. And she rarely banged her head against the wall the way she used to when she was younger.

She turned her face to the rec room ceiling, and crowed.

*

Another round of snow; I'd lost count. Dad must have towed twenty cars out of ditches and drifts. Lissy's boot prints in the backyard looked like Speedy Gonzales trying to take all four directions at the same time. On the evening of the worst storm, Dad and I threw snow over our heads, to the towering banks on both sides of the driveway. "You'd think God was putting a new twist on the old flood," he said, tossing shovelfuls of snow over the hedge, the crabapple tree growing shorter by the minute.

Amazing how one snowfall can have so many meanings. For me it was an adventure. I'd pictured igloos everywhere, imagined ice sculptures of Abraham Lincoln sitting on his presidential throne, or Marilyn Monroe trying to keep her dress from blowing up around her thighs. For Lissy it was one big playground. She'd slid in the snow, rolled over it, flung it up into the air. For Mom it was a change of scenery, another channel, and she'd pressed her face to the front window to watch us each time we shovelled, half-smiling.

For Dad it was mumbled curses and numb hands, his misery fascinating not only to me but to the whole of Arizona Avenue. He'd witnessed every snowstorm over the last forty-six years and was completely unimpressed. Snow was backbreaking and boring: the hard truth. The other men on the street didn't have my father's single-mindedness. They suffered quietly.

They inched their way toward us, slyly urging Dad to complain.

"How's it going, Ed?" Mr. Burr asked.

"Yeah, how do you like this snow?" Mr. Milford, who'd been struggling with cancer since last spring, had shuffled across the street in order not to miss one of Dad's famous epithets. Lonny Milford leaned on his shovel to listen. Mr. Costello, carrying his bottle of beer, joined the small crowd of men eager to shake their fists at a sky that never emptied.

"How do I like this?" Dad asked. "I'd rather have a plague of frogs."

"Damn right." Mr. Costello nodded.

"You slave all day trying to get a little money into your pocket, and what for?"

No one responded. No one seemed to know.

"So you can come home to your hard-earned house and find that a bloody avalanche is standing between you and your front door."

"Don't I know it," Mr. Burr agreed, slapping his gloves together.

"It's like digging a tunnel through the Rocky Mountains," Dad continued. "The whole winter long. And then come summer, you've got grass up to your ass, not to mention enough wormy crabapples to feed an army."

"Then those blasted leaves in the fall," Mr. Milford added.

"Don't get me started on leaves," Dad said. "In October, I'd like to torch the entire neighbourhood."

"Boom!" Lonny Milford mimed lighting a match and tossing it into an invisible pile of leaves.

★

Next morning I was in agony. The muscles in my upper arms and the backs of my legs throbbed. Despite the pain, I had to honour the promise I'd made to help Lissy build a snowman in the backyard. I tried to persuade Mom to join us, but she didn't even bother to dream up an excuse.

Lissy's ideas about how to build a snowman were different from mine, but since it was Lissy's project, it seemed wise to let her do whatever she wanted. Instead of the usual giant snowball base, Lissy piled up a hodgepodge of snow and patted it down until it was hard enough to bear her weight. Same thing with the second level, except the mound was taller and dangerously crooked.

"It might fall down," I warned, but Lissy heaved a shoulder against it to prove it was solid. Astonishingly, it stayed in place, like the Leaning Tower of Pisa. When it came to the head, Lissy hand-packed several ordinary-sized snowballs, but rejected them one by one. I made snowballs too, holding them up for her approval. She either shook her head vigorously or knocked them right out of my hand. Finally, one of my snowballs succeeded. She grabbed it, squashing it on top of the Leaning Tower, squealing with satisfaction. It looked a little bizarre, but it was original. Linda Burr and the Remington twins had each made a snowman and you couldn't tell them apart; it was like they'd been poured from a mould. Lissy might not have been much of a thinker, but at least she wasn't a copycat.

"What do you want to use for eyes?"

"No. Red red red." She held her red scarf up to her own mouth.

"You've got to have eyes, Lissy. Otherwise the snowman won't be able to see."

"Red," she insisted.

"I don't see any red." I pointed at several bushes and trees.

"Red," she said more loudly, clutching her scarf as if she might rip it into shreds.

I tried to think fast. If Lissy ended up in tears, running inside to Mom, I'd be the one to blame. I leaned over and pretended to kiss the snowball. Smack. Smooch. I made the wettest sound I could.

"There," I said, "it's got a red mouth now." I had to repeat the whole thing twice more before Lissy caught on. She screamed her happy scream. She must have kissed the snowball fifty times.

The Milfords, the Remingtons, the Burrs and the Costellos all had their own twisted warps, but no other family on the block had a Lissy to contend with, or a father whose bad moods could be so charismatic, or a mother who was pretty much under a house arrest of her own devising. Not one of the other families on Arizona Avenue had an eyeless, pinheaded snowman with an invisible mouthful of kisses.

*

The day before my birthday, I was in a state of anticipation so heightened it felt like anxiety. Deep inside my thirteen-year-old body, growing larger and larger as the hours ticked by, a fourteen-year-old stranger was stretching my bones, spreading my skin. By nighttime, I thought I was going to burst.

The morning of January seventeenth, I decorated the rec room. I lugged down my portable record player, put out bowls of Cheezies and barbecue chips. This was to be my first all-friends birthday party. Marco told me that he'd overheard a couple of the invited boys wondering out loud whether their parents would allow them to attend a party at a retard's house. But Marco thought it was probably a joke and I didn't want him to think that stuff like this actually worried me.

Dad had to work and Mom said she was too shy to face such a big crowd of strange boys alone, so Grammie was the designated chaperon, plus Aunt Veronica and Uncle Maurice. My cousin Roma would be the only girl.

"Roma will make good company for Lissy," Grammie said, refusing to pick favourites amongst her grandchildren. She was wearing one of her usual old lady dresses, but her shoes looked like she could have walked across Siberia in them, and her thick, short-cropped hair reminded me of the helmet Sergeant Schultz wore on *Hogan's Heroes*. These past few months she'd been spending more and more time at our place, bossing me around. She had arrived before noon with my gift, a hideous blue plaid suit jacket, not even wrapped.

Fat-faced, long-nosed Roma was, of course, the first young person to arrive.

"Where did you get those?" she asked, pointing at the paisley streamers criss-crossing the rec room ceiling. Her voice was like maple syrup squirting from a water gun. Without waiting for a response, she started poking through my record collection.

Marco arrived next, banging his feet as he came down the basement stairs, with Lissy right behind him.

The next fifteen minutes were a blur, fighting to keep Lissy from stealing handfuls of snacks from every bowl in the room and enduring Roma's endless snobbishness. "On my fourteenth birthday..." she kept bragging to Marco, exaggerating how Leo-the-lion-like it all was, from the matching gold and green decorations to the over twenty kids who attended. At the end of the first hour only two more guests had arrived: Louie Burr, from across the street, and Dana Toad, a boy who was actually more Marco's friend than mine. By this time, I'd stopped bothering with Lissy, letting her eat as she pleased. Roma ignored us, playing Sonny and

Cher's "I Got You Babe" and singing the Sonny part with a gruff, put-on voice then switching to a bored soprano for Cher's lines. My mother was hiding in her bedroom.

Aunt Veronica, who always looked like one of those well-dressed women in the Eaton's catalogue, not a hair out of place and exactly the right amount of rouge, served the hot dogs and potato salad. She had gigantic tears in the corners of her eyes as she passed around the mustard. I had a sneaking suspicion that Marco's warning was correct, and none of the other invited boys would be coming. Aunt Veronica, always a sucker for a sob story, was feeling sorry for me.

Uncle Maurice, the alderman, plopped down into an armchair. "There's been some phone calls, some cancellations," he said, rubbing a fist into the palm of his other hand.

I could feel Roma's eyes on me. And I knew that if I even looked at Marco, he'd say what he'd overheard at school. "Who cares," I said.

"So, on with the show?" Uncle Maurice looked relieved. "What sort of games have you got planned? How about pin the tail on the ass?" he joked, lifting his right hip into the air.

"This isn't a kid's party," I said. "I'm fourteen years old."

"On my birthday we played charades," Roma bragged. "Like at a cocktail party."

"You've been to a cocktail party?" Marco asked, his cheeks stuffed with hot dog.

"I've seen them on TV," Roma said.

"We don't have a TV," Dana Toad whispered.

Uncle Maurice cut Dana off with a bellow, reaching out and grabbing Lissy by the back of her yellow party dress. "Pin the tail on the Lissy," he said, tickling her. "Who's first?"

"She's not a party game," I yelled.

"What is she?" Dana asked, genuinely curious.

"She's a sister," I snapped. "A retarded sister."

"Retarded has nothing to do with it." Uncle Maurice was trying to soothe us all. He pulled Lissy into his arms for another hug to prove she was neither dangerous nor contagious.

"Yeah, there's nothing wrong with retarded," Marco said, patting my arm, leaving a light green relish stain on my white shirt. It was the pat that pushed me over the edge.

"Fuck," I said. My hands were shaking so much I couldn't wipe away the tears.

"Are you crying?" Dana Toad asked, puckering up his own face as if he was going to join in.

"Ignorant people don't know what retarded is," Uncle Maurice said.

"Who?" Roma asked, her nose in everything.

"The ignorant jerks not at this party," Marco answered.

Before any more questions could be asked, before I could figure out who to be furious at, Aunt Veronica came bursting back in with my birthday cake. I saw my mother standing outside the room, looking freaked out, as if three times the number of invited kids had showed up and were in the process of taking over her house.

★

I woke up next day feeling nauseous and decided on my own to stay home from school. There were five classmates whose excuses I didn't want to hear.

After a day of *Let's Make a Deal, The Price Is Right, The Mike Douglas Show* and *The Dating Game*, I called Marco.

"How come your Mom lets you use the phone when you're sick?"

"Why shouldn't she?"

"My Mom stays home from work when I'm sick. She's pretty paranoid that I might be faking. She does everything she can to punish me: castor oil, horse pills, even asshole thermometers."

My mother liked my company, even when I was sullen. I lay on the rec room couch and she sat quietly in the armchair next to me, with the fold-up card table near at hand, knitting, polishing the silver, sewing buttons, writing cheques. Lissy was okay with my bad mood, sprawled on the rug, playing with some of my birthday presents, especially the pair of electric-blue suspenders that snapped like huge elastic bands. Even Queen Mary, our twenty-pound, ten-year-old Persian cat, stuck close to me all day, choosing my lap as her throne, dozing through most of the shows, except for the back-to-back *I Love Lucy* episodes, when she stared right at the TV, purring so loud my mother had to turn up the sound.

The next day I went back to school wearing a Perry Mason stone face, showing those guys who had tried to ruin my birthday how little they mattered. I flashed them the same sort of look Bachelor number three had given the unlucky Bachelorette who'd made the mistake of picking ugly Bachelor number one over him.

*

Aunt Ruby, my mother's other sister, the cool one in the family, and her husband Frank, who looked like a cross between Eddy Arnold and Elvis Presley, were the best. Uncle Frank was a country and western singer who called himself Frankie Wilde. One of his songs, "Tearjerker," was actually played on the radio. Aunt Ruby was concentrating most of her spare energy on Uncle Frank's career, but had plans to open her own nightclub one day. She was a part-time secretary for an insurance company, but that didn't diminish her ambition.

For a belated birthday present, they took me to The Brown Derby to hear Uncle Frank perform. Aunt Ruby and I sat at a table right in front of the stage. She was wearing a dark red dress with skinny shoulder straps and a matching satin bow in her midnight-black hair. Every time Uncle Frank was applauded, he leaned down and grinned at us, the sequins on his cowboy shirt throwing tiny glints all over our table.

Aunt Ruby danced with me several times before twirling me into the arms of complete strangers, each one prettier than the one before. The palms of my hands smelled like a mix of Chanel No. 5 and beer. Uncle Frank dedicated "Moon River" to me. I was drunk on all the attention.

"Was it dreamy, or what?" Aunt Ruby crooned as we drove home.

"Or what," I agreed.

"But was it as good as your rootin'-tootin' party?" Uncle Frank asked.

"Oh, that," I said. "Even the dentist would have been more fun." When I told them what had actually happened, they were both quiet for a minute.

"Why didn't Maurice or Veronica tell us?" Uncle Frank finally asked.

"For heaven's sake, Frank, Maurice and Veronica never talk about anything other than themselves." Aunt Ruby turned herself completely around until she was on her knees, leaning over into the back seat. She took hold of my face with both her hands and kissed me lightly on the tip of my nose. "People can be really cruel sometimes."

"I know," I said, hoping that I wasn't going to start crying again.

"What's going on, Robby? Is your mother okay?"

"I guess so."

"Is she getting out much?"

"Not too much."

"Never?"

"Sort of," I said. I could hardly sit still. A part of me was squirming to confess everything, to say out loud that something was terribly wrong.

She gave me her great lipstick grin. "She's getting housebound. I'll fix that. Grammie used to call her a little mouse when we were kids. Little mouse hiding all day in the house."

When they dropped me off at home, I waddled like Charlie Chaplin up the steps to the front door to draw their attention away from the living room window where the drapes were moving ever so slightly.

★

I love the clatter of Kingston Road Public School's steamy radiators the same way I love Rice Krispies for breakfast, Campbell's tomato soup at lunch, "O Canada" over the morning intercom, my evening bath, Dad's snoring, Marco's recess hoots, my mother's soaps and the width of my navy blue ballpoint. But the good stuff evaporated when I arrived home the next afternoon to find my mother talking on the kitchen telephone, squeezed between the table and the wall.

"I am not…well, that's absurd," she was saying, her voice an octave higher than usual. "It was a lovely party. If only I had the time, I'd have lunch downtown at least once a week."

I stood nervously at the door of the kitchen, snow melting all over the floor. "The floor," she blurted, dropping the phone into its cradle and grabbing a handful of paper towel.

"You are the height of rudeness, Robinson Tedley," she muttered as she worked. "Telling Aunt Ruby all those private things."

"I didn't tell her anything except about *my* party."

"Half the world's starving, Robinson, and you're whining about having a smaller party than the Prince of Wales."

"I wasn't whining, I was explaining what happened."

Having sponged sufficiently around me, she started to unzip my coat and untangle my scarf, like I was four instead of fourteen. "And what's this about me never going outside? Aunt Ruby should have had kids, she's got too much time on her hands."

"What are you blaming me for?" I asked. "It's Aunt Ruby who's worried about you, not me."

"Well, thanks for nothing," she said, almost pulling my arms out of their sockets as she yanked off my coat. "What does she know about my life?"

I had a sinking feeling that this was the beginning of a lecture. "So start going out more," I said. "Go all the way to India," I added, "and phone Aunt Ruby from the Taj Mahal."

"I might just do that."

She was calming down, finally letting me into the kitchen in my stocking feet.

"Sky is another word for outer space," she said, nodding, as if it might make a good opening argument with Aunt Ruby somewhere down the line. "It goes on and on and it makes me dizzy. I prefer a roof. Is there anything wrong with that?"

"But we're not going to float away."

"I wouldn't be so sure!" she said. She turned aside, grabbing the damp dishcloth and wiping the already sparkling kitchen counter.

"There," she said as if she'd accomplished something. "Let's join Lissy and catch the tail end of *The Secret Storm*. Those people have real problems."

TWO

A FEW DAYS LATER, I came straight home from school to find Aunt Ruby's car in the driveway and our front door partially open. Aunt Ruby was planted in the middle of the living room, still wearing her honey-coloured mink jacket, red-painted fingernails, arms akimbo. She was staring at my mother, cowered in the armchair furthest from the window, an elastic bandage prominent around her right ankle. Apparently Aunt Ruby had called my mother, inviting her out to Watt's Restaurant for afternoon tea and refusing to take no for an answer. When she tooted her horn, my mother stood inside the front storm door, lifting up the bandaged foot.

"You're a lost cause." Aunt Ruby, angry, was nasty and elegant. No doubt the meanness had been inherited from Grammie, but the elegance was all her own.

"Accidents happen," my mother said. She looked right through me, not even noticing that I'd entered the room. "I was sweeping off the back porch and, boom, I slipped on a patch of ice."

"What's come over you, Flo? The world doesn't bite."

"My world is fine and dandy, thank you very much. When I want to go out on the back porch, I go. And when I have a hankering for Watt's, I'll go there too."

"So this is stubbornness. Is that what you're saying?" Aunt

Ruby was a whiz at finding cracks in flimsy arguments.

"I'm saying that my ankle is sprained and that's that."

"What do you say, Robby?" Aunt Ruby asked. "Don't you think your mother spends too much time indoors?"

"This isn't indoors," Mom interrupted, shifting her position so she was sitting more defiantly, her right ankle held carefully off the floor, "this is my home."

"Whatever you call it, Flo, you've had this problem for a long time. And it's getting worse. Now even Robby's affected by it."

"Is that true, Robinson?" she asked, out-glaring Aunt Ruby.

I had no idea what to say; the truth had no more to do with me than with Jack Frost or Sandra Dee. I knew Aunt Ruby was right, but also that whatever was wrong with my mother couldn't be corrected as easily as a trip to Watt's.

"It's good to get fresh air," I said.

"Exactly," Aunt Ruby agreed, turning toward my mother, then back to me.

Sinking deep into the armchair, my mother's anger dissolved. "You might as well throw me into Lake Ontario," she said at last, the last three syllables mangled together in a sob.

Aunt Ruby softened. She ran her right hand down the left sleeve of her mink jacket then bent to stroke my mother's hair. "You're not alone. Flo. I've been watching out for you ever since we were girls."

Just then Dad appeared in the doorway. Friday afternoon was his early dinner break. "What's going on?"

"Your wife has a serious problem. She can't even go to Watt's anymore."

Mom launched into her side of the story, still sniffling, showing off her ankle. "Don't you think I'd rather have a nice Watt's cup of tea instead of excruciating pain?"

"What you'd rather and what you're capable of are two different things," Aunt Ruby said.

"Where's Lissy?" Dad asked, the subject not only changed but flipped.

"In the rec room," Mom said, "watching TV."

He turned to Aunt Ruby. "How can you expect Flo to prance out for afternoon tea and leave Lissy all alone?"

"We weren't leaving until Robby came home."

"Robby has homework and chores."

"For the love of Pete." Aunt Ruby exploded. "We're talking about Flo's mental health, not her motherly duties. Forget Watt's, how about a walk around the block?"

Dad's body stiffened. "You think I work like a dog so my wife can sashay around the block with her nothing-to-do-all-day sister? You're living the easy life, Ruby. Type a little in the morning and play all afternoon." His lips froze for a second in a sneer. "Flo goes outside when there's outside work to be done. She gets the week's groceries, takes Lissy for walks, sweeps the back porch."

"Oh, Ed," Aunt Ruby said, her voice threadbare. "Even Robby knows there's a problem. Isn't that right, Robby?"

"Enough is enough." Dad waved one greasy hand in the direction of the front door. "People solve their own problems when they're good and ready. Go mind somebody else's business."

"Okay. I'm not going to keep banging my head against the wall." Aunt Ruby was biting her bottom lip.

There was total silence for a few moments, then some awkward small talk, Mom and Aunt Ruby going through the motions of making up. Dad fixed his eyes on a neutral corner of the room. Aunt Ruby looked fierce as she headed for the door, stopping to kiss me on the cheek, pinching up a bit of skin on my wrist between her dark nails.

As the roar of her car faded, Dad stared at Mom for a second, then started for the kitchen. "Come on, Robby. We've got dinner to make."

"Don't make me feel guilty about dinner." Mom tried to look haughty but was too pale to pull it off.

A tiny tremor passed across Dad's face, but when he spoke he sounded perfectly calm. "You take care of that sore ankle, Flo." It didn't escape me that the word "sore" was miles away from "twisted" or "sprained." Dad knew a bit about the power of language.

*

I felt restless the next day, so it was easy for Marco to talk me into trying to sneak a look through the tall windows of Kingdom Hall where the Remington twins went to worship. Marco had a crush on Franny, although half the time it seemed to me that he was actually lusting after Lucy. Beneath the window I linked my hands together for Marco to step into and boosted him until he was able to grab the sill and gain some extra leverage. He started babbling about seeing all sorts of lurid stuff—the minister jerking off behind the pulpit while women sat in the pews naked from the waist up—so I dropped my hands and he slid down the brick wall, scraping his palms.

"It's my turn," I insisted, but as I was stepping into his hands, two old guys hustled around the corner of the building, shouting at us. Marco dropped me on my ass and took off. I managed to roll out of reach and dash after him, leaving the two guys behind after half a block.

I spent the next couple of days waiting for a big black sedan to pull up beside me on my walk home from school and drag me off for some horrifying Jehovah's Witness torture. Marco started spreading stories around school that we'd seen weird devil worship rituals involving Franny's naked body. It was a relief to come home and find Aunt Veronica baking Valentine's Day cookies with my mother. Her chatter never amounted to much, but like fairy tales her stories were strangely comforting.

"You should have seen the table, Flo. Festooned with enough silverware to fill a pirate's treasure chest. And the hors d'oeuvres were almost too gorgeous to eat. I turned to Madge Crawley, you know, the mayor's sister-in-law with the peach-coloured hair, and said 'Go ahead and *try* telling me I haven't died and gone to heaven.'"

I basked in the smell of warm gingerbread and the music of Aunt Veronica's voice: dinner parties she'd been invited to, the ins and outs of renting a rug shampooer. Lissy was sitting at the kitchen table, her eyes glazed. I stopped listening and allowed the rhythm of the words to become a pleasant buzz. Even my mother seemed blissful, as if she'd found a safe way to leave the house.

★

In a pre-Valentine's good mood, Miss Luther gave me a new topic for independent study: the President of the United States, Lyndon Baines Johnson. I'd had no idea that a leader of a country could look and act like LBJ. Oak-tree tall and weathered, beefy and surly. He looked like he could pick Indira Gandhi up with his baby finger. Like he'd never give in to anyone, no matter what was at stake. I could have kept on reading about him for hours, but Miss Luther announced that it was time for our annual Valentine's bash, with chocolate milk and cupcakes with red Cupids pressed into the icing. Did LBJ send Lady Bird a mushy card showing two doves pecking at one other?

Marco had a chocolate moustache and was flirting with every girl in the class. Dana Toad asked Miss Luther to dance to "Puppet on a String." Louie Burr composed a pornographic Valentine to send to four-eyed Ginny Tucker. Wendy Fergie marched up to the turntable and set Petula Clark's "My Love" spinning, then made a beeline for my desk and dragged me onto the makeshift dance floor. Despite the fast tempo, Wendy insisted we dance slow, her hands leading me, her right hand clasping my left with a powerful grip. When the song was over, she leaned in and kissed me on the lips.

I didn't have a clue how to react. Wasn't there a law against kissing in a grade eight classroom? My groin reacted. I was afraid to look around in case everyone was staring. Wendy blushed and sighed like someone being burnt at the stake and actually enjoying the flames. "Excuse me," I said, backing away and banging into the blackboard.

When it came time to exchange cards, was I imagining it, or did the other girls in the class hand me their pink envelopes with subtle shrugs of apology? Wendy Fergie had laid her claim. Her Valentine showed two puppies rolling over one another. The caption: *I'm doggone crazy about you.* Was this what my mother experienced when Aunt Ruby threatened her with a trip to Watt's for tea? Was this what Dad meant when he said the world was always thinking up new ways to torture him? Was this what LBJ felt when he worried about the Viet Cong breathing down his neck?

★

The next day, Saturday, Dad dragged himself home from the Texaco, the wrinkles on his brow squeezed hard. At dinnertime I pulled out my chair at the table, but he stood up abruptly, almost knocking his chair over.

"Downstairs, Robby," he snapped. "Now."

He led me into the laundry room, and I stood between the washer and the dryer under the bare light bulb. He leaned his weight against the washer, fixed me with an I-already-know-you're-guilty stare and said, "What's this I hear about you spreading vicious rumours about the Remingtons?"

Fucking Marco, blabbing his lies. "I don't think you've got the story straight," I said.

"Mr. Burr filled me in while I was changing his oil," he said. "Mr. Burr's a cop. Facts are his business."

"I'm sorry," I said. "I was curious. I didn't know Marco's stories were going to get out of hand."

"Don't swing the blame. No son of mine is going to be too willy-nilly to face the music."

"Yes, sir."

"Jehovah's Witnesses don't fornicate with the devil. They don't slime themselves with feces and swing from chandeliers. They don't have smoke pouring from their ears. They don't eat live kittens. Am I clearer than clear?"

I tried to interrupt. Not even Marco's imagination was that wild.

"No buts, not one," he said. "Don't you realize I've got enough problems without you turning into a juvenile delinquent."

"I'm sorry," I repeated, "but I've never even heard those gross stories before."

"Well, you're hearing them now. The fruit of your little adventure," he said. "Let this be a lesson. If you say yuck, someone else will come along and say double yuck. What starts out as a fib, ends up slander."

I nodded.

"That's it for melodrama, you hear me," he said. "After dinner you apologize to the Remingtons and we can all get back to normal."

Less than half an hour later, bits of pork chop still stuck between my teeth, I strode across the street. *Suspect pressing doorbell. Suspect pausing on porch. Suspect entering house.*

"Well, look who's here." Franny and Lucy both giggled, already enjoying themselves. I wouldn't put it past them to exaggerate Marco's stories themselves, just for the pleasure of watching me squirm.

"I came to apologize for all those things I didn't actually say. They're still my fault, of course."

They responded with two noncommittal Okays, but gave each other the tiniest wink.

"I have to apologize to your mother too," I explained, figuring this was where I'd be forced to sing a hymn or conk myself on the head.

"She's in the bathtub," Franny said, and Lucy added, "You'll have to shout."

"Shout?"

"Shout you're sorry."

It felt like being forced to swallow a lump of phlegm.

"I'm sorry, Mrs. Remington," I yelled.

"Okay," they both said again.

"Okay," I repeated. "See you around?"

"Just a second," Lucy said, while Franny turned and glanced down the hall. "We need to ask you a question."

"Sure."

They looked at one another, and Lucy asked, "Which one of us did you imagine naked?"

This was to be my humiliation, like being forced to stand up in class with a boner.

"I... ah... I thought I saw..." It wasn't really shyness that was holding me back. In fact I felt a kind of flush go through my body that wasn't at all unpleasant. I had an overwhelming desire to somehow keep this feeling going. "Well, actually," I started over, "I imagined both of you."

They exchanged another look, and then let me go. No more questions, no recriminations.

Was it possible I had actually pleased the Remington twins? I seemed to be entering a phase of my life where absolutely nothing would make sense.

★

In February, the icicles hanging from the eavestrough started dripping non-stop. Snowbanks shrank before my eyes. Marco, Louie, Dana Toad and I splashed around in my backyard, pretending the Mississippi River had overflowed. I was supposed to be watching Lissy too, but since Linda Burr and Barfy were hanging out in the driveway, I figured Lissy was being entertained enough to stay put.

I heard a muffled pounding. My mother was banging on the back door window, trying to get my attention, me up to my ankles in melted snow, jeans sopping wet. By the time I'd sloshed my way to the back porch, Mom was frantic. "Where's Melissa?" she said. "You've let her get away."

Lissy had always gone through spells where she'd wander away (or *escape* as Grammie liked to call it). She could run like a racehorse in a direction impossible to anticipate. I seem to have a memory of my mother high-kneeing it after her back in the day when she was still going outside. But it was definitely my responsibility this time. Just the thought of Dad's anger made me queasy. I enlisted Marco, Louie and Dana Toad as a posse. Matter of life and death, I said.

"What do I do if I find her?" Dana asked nervously.

"Promise her chocolate cake."

I headed for Kingston Road, counting on Lissy's love of bustle to lead her toward the sound of traffic. If she'd chosen side streets, she might wander into any old backyard with an open gate or something furry, a squirrel or a cat.

I ran in and out of every store: the Chinese variety, the barbershop, the hardware, the bakery, even the shoe repair. When I passed the Texaco, I tried to will myself invisible, hoping my mother hadn't called Dad.

In and out, in and out, I weaved my way through the steamy aisles of the laundromat, the always slightly stinky pet store, the glistening druggist's and the hairdressing salon that smelled of hairspray. At the fabric store a woman with a blue rinse hairdo swore she'd been staring out the window for hours and would have noticed a retarded girl. I checked the grocery store, from the bins of vegetables to the rows of neatly stacked canned goods, then on to the library, both the children and adult rooms.

At Carolina Crescent, I headed north again, back into the maze of small streets with their lineups of identical bungalows. Enough time had passed since my mother's first panic. She was sure to have telephoned Dad by now. I turned east at the western end of Dakota Drive and began calling Lissy's name, whistling too. Two blocks away from Arizona Avenue, I caught a glimpse of Dana disappearing behind a spindly hedge. A second later he emerged, tugging Lissy by the sleeves of her winter coat.

Of course Lissy didn't have a moment's guilt. To her the world was wonderful. Mom met her at the door with a huge hug, while I was met by Dad, forced home in the middle of a workday, a busy day as always, a day that I had ruined.

"Can't I trust you at all?" He slapped me across my face, something he'd never done before. Despite the sting, I didn't reach up to touch my cheek. He rubbed at his chest as if trying to erase something, inhaling so deeply I could feel the weight of his breath. He left the house then, climbed into the tow truck, tore backwards onto the street, tires spraying slush as he screeched away.

*

My nightmare was about a giant truck lumbering toward me, so the first cry sounded dream-like. What finally woke me was the hall light shining across my bed. Mom was standing in my doorway, her hair frizzed out. "Help me, Robby," she said in a tone strangely flat. "He can hardly breathe."

I stumbled to my feet. The legs of my pajamas were twisted at the knee and practically cutting off my circulation. Then I heard the cry again, this time clearly coming from my parent's bedroom. I heard the word *Fuck* plain as day, Dad's voice but bent out of shape.

He was doubled over a chair, clutching at his chest. His cheeks were blue.

"I can't breathe," he sputtered.

In the kitchen, the moon-faced clock over the fridge showed 3 AM. I only knew a couple of phone numbers off by heart. I was sure Dad wouldn't want Aunt Ruby involved, and Marco's parents couldn't even speak English. That left Louie Burr. Of course: a cop, perfect. After a couple of rings, Mr. Burr answered.

"It's Robinson Tedley," I said. Nothing but the facts. "I think my father's having a heart attack."

All I had to do was obey Mr. Burr. *Open the front door for the ambulance. Tell your mother to get dressed and keep watch over your father. Tell him to hang in there.*

It was only a matter of minutes before the street was screaming with sirens, the ambulance and a police car arriving together. In the bedroom, a transparent oxygen mask was strapped to Dad's face and two attendants lifted him onto a stretcher. The policemen were surprisingly young and frightened-looking. They paced the length of the hall, overseeing everything. Mr. Burr was outside, directing traffic in a pair of prison-striped blue pajamas and a ratty button-down sweater.

When they carried Dad out into the ambulance, the street was ablaze with light, faces pressed up against lit windows.

"Daddy?" Lissy walked into the living room, her hands fluttering in the air. Mom gathered her into her arms.

One of the policemen cocked his head and cleared his throat to get Mom's attention.

"Ma'am?" He reached out and tapped her free shoulder. "I just wanted to say that you're allowed to ride with the ambulance. Is there someone I can call to stay with your kids?"

The pink of her cheeks had faded. She burrowed more tightly into Lissy. "I can't leave my daughter with just anyone."

The policeman nodded and left. A few minutes later, Dad was whisked off alone into the night.

"What if he needs us?" I asked. "He'll think we've abandoned him."

Hurt flashed across my Mom's face.

"How can you talk like that? He'll be able to concentrate on getting better, knowing that things are the way they should be at home."

She patted Lissy on the head a few times then gave her a bear hug.

"Back to bed now," she ordered. "Tomorrow will be here before we know it." She seemed relieved that Dad was gone. Although it seemed thoughtless to think of sleep while my father struggled for his life a few miles away, eventually I faded out and dreamt about him lifting boulders from our driveway and tossing them up into the sky.

*

As soon as I woke up I headed straight to Lissy's room.

"Get dressed," I ordered, fumbling in her closet, throwing a pair of corduroy pants and a white fisherman's sweater on the bed. "We're going to see Dad."

Mom was already dressed, sitting in the kitchen, one hand resting on the phone. "I've called everyone," she said. "Everyone knows."

"What about the hospital?" I pictured East General rather than my father's body, rust-red bricks, not blue skin.

"Resting comfortably," Mom said, lifting her fingers from the phone one at a time and one at a time dropping them down again. "Comfortable," she repeated. "That's not too bad."

She sounded like a weather report. It must be shock, I thought. I'd heard about people paralyzed in pools of blood or on window ledges twenty storeys up. She was holding the telephone tight, as if it were Dad's hand. I couldn't think of anything to say. He might as well have been shipped to Calcutta.

I grabbed the Yellow Pages from the top shelf of the broom closet. Tailors, tarpaulins, tattooing, tax, taxidermists, taxis.

"Lissy and I are going to the hospital," I said.

Mom sat quietly while I spoke to the East End Taxi Company. She didn't budge when I left the room to dress. When I returned, half-buttoned up, her lips looked like she was posed for a photo.

"What do I say if he wakes up and asks for you?" I said, trying Grammie's guilt strategy. Somewhere inside her shock, she had to be feeling awful.

"He needs to rest, not visit," she said. It sounded like her tongue was taped to the roof of her mouth.

"He needs to know we're there. What'll I tell Aunt Ruby if she shows up?"

Aunt Ruby's name was like a small string of firecrackers going off. Mom's face twitched in five or six different places.

"And how do you suggest I do it?" I could hear the panic. She looked at me as if I might have the answer. "How do I get there and back alive?"

I couldn't go to the hospital without her. It was totally clear to me that if she stayed home now, she would never go outside again.

"You can wear Dad's green parka over your own coat, the one with the hood, and a pair of earmuffs. I'll tie a scarf across your face. You can wear sunglasses. You won't even feel the air."

I didn't wait for her to object. I simply started dressing her. By the time the cab arrived, she looked like an Arctic explorer. The nine steps to the taxi were nine of the stiffest, heaviest, scariest steps she had ever walked. I could hear her crying beneath all those layers. Lissy helped—she thought we were playing a great new game. We each took a well-padded arm and maneuvered her as best we could. Safe in the back seat, she slouched low, pressing gloves firmly against the sunglasses.

We got her without mishap to Dad's room in intensive care, and after that she was able to fake it. She stood inside the room, peeling off most of the extra clothes and leaving them in a pile behind the open door. She leaned over the hospital bed and looked into Dad's grey face. He looked back, not bothering to hide his surprise. He turned his tired gaze on me, and I saw a whole bunch of emotions slipping one into another. But he was too weak to talk.

Lissy played with the bars at the foot of the bed. I stood across from Mom with hands at my sides, letting everything that had happened roll through me, wishing that the crisis was over and that we could all stay there in the ICU with all its miraculous machines, canisters of oxygen and people paid to keep us alive.

Aunt Veronica and Uncle Maurice were the next to arrive, followed less than ten minutes later by Aunt Ruby and Uncle Frank. Aunt Ruby spent most of her time staring at Mom as if she were seeing a hired look-alike. Mr. and Mrs. Burr showed up too, but they didn't seem to notice anything out of the ordinary.

The three of us hung around long after everyone else had gone. It was way after dark before Dad fell asleep. When one of the nurses told us it was time to go home, I quietly bundled my mother up again. "Abominable Snowman," she said, brushing a strand of hair from my forehead before putting on her gloves.

As we rode home in the back of the cab, it struck me that the shapeless heap of winter clothes squeezed between Lissy and me was not the same mother who, just a year earlier, could trim the boxwood hedge and hose down the sidewalk until it gleamed. I remembered her playing a crazy game of badminton with Lissy, leaping into the air to swing at the birdie. We used to sit on the back steps together after dinner, sunbathing with our eyes closed, telling each other about the blazes behind our lids. The terrified creature sitting between Lissy and me was an imposter. By the time we arrived at Arizona Avenue, I knew I was going to have to struggle to get my normal mother back. In the house, when Lissy and I unwound her from the layers of jacket, sweater and scarf, I was surprised to see how much like her old self she looked. She was so glad to be home that she walked from room to room, admiring everything. But soon enough she ended up in her chair by the window, peering out.

"Next time will be even easier," I said, breaking the silence.

"If you only knew," she said, showing me the tiny space between index finger and thumb. "I came this close to dying out there on those awful streets."

That gave me chills. "Dad's the one who almost died," I said. Didn't she know that?

"We're all hanging on between life and death."

"So hang on tighter," I said. "I mean it," I added, but she didn't appear to be listening. She seemed to be mesmerized by something invisible in the dark.

*

I was beginning to wonder if the world really spun, or whether it flipped every now and again, a somersault. Head-over-heels. One day my feet were flat on the ground, the next I was hanging from the ceiling like a bat.

The following afternoon Aunt Ruby and Uncle Frank took me to see Dad. He was propped up in bed, grinning, talking a mile a minute.

"Boy, what an experience," he boasted. "I saw stars *and* my whole life passed before my eyes. My chest felt like Queen Mary was digging her claws right into my heart. All I could think about was that my last day on earth had been wasted at bloody Texaco."

I'd never seen him so excited. On the drive home Aunt Ruby suggested that this attack might be one of those heavily disguised blessings Grammie was always talking about.

"It got Flo out of the house and Ed out of the Texaco. If that's not a miracle, then I'm an escargot."

Back home, my mother was still in her nightgown and the oversized green terrycloth robe that made her look like a bushy shrub. She had "the worst flu this side of Hong Kong." Her only acknowledgement of me was to warn me to keep my distance. I could have the rec room all to myself.

Grammie in charge was like playing house with someone so bossy that all Lissy and I were expected to do was obey orders. "I'm not leaving till this household is back on its feet again," she declared. She had already rearranged the glasses and cups cupboard, an accident-waiting-to-happen whenever Lissy reached behind a row of breakable juice glasses to retrieve her favourite plastic cup, the one with puppies on it.

"Count yourself lucky, young man," Grammie said to my frown. "I lost my father when I was twelve and was sent out to work the very next day, sewing bows and flowers on fancy hats." When I forgot to wipe up the crumbs after making myself a honey sandwich, she shouted, "What did your last servant die of? God did not put me on this earth to wait on the likes of you." The complaints escalated as the evening progressed. Finally, I ended up on the couch doing absolutely nothing, just about afraid to breathe, a perfect vantage point from which to watch Grammie baby my mother, doing everything short of blowing her nose and scolding her for minor infractions: flipping through a *Reader's Digest* magazine without her reading glasses and not putting the right amount of Vaseline on her chapped nose.

If I were my mother, I'd be much more afraid of Grammie

than the sky. But by bedtime, she seemed younger than I'd ever seen her before. Lissy was playing with a pile of stuffed toys. She cried when Grammie tried to limit the number she could take to bed with her. The last thing Grammie said to me was "Have you brushed your teeth?" When I nodded, she said, "Prove it." I bared them, top and bottom.

*

Aunt Ruby made one of her spectacular entrances, mink coat wide open, displaying a purple movie star silk blouse and a wide patent leather belt. She was brandishing a bag of goodies for my mother, including a tin of Sucrets, three butter-coloured lemons, a big bottle of ginger ale and the latest *Modern Screen* and *Chatelaine*.

Before I was even properly awake, Aunt Ruby had me buckled into the front seat of her car. The stark winter trees, the dingy pockets of snow, none of it had any effect on her blissful mood. "*Just one look was all it took,*" she sang, pounding my knee until I started to hum along.

The hospital was full of activity. Dad's skin was positively shiny.

"Crank me up," he said, adopting a pirate's salty accent. "This here bed can do everything but fly."

Where were his miseries, his complaints? With his heart attack he was beaming right before my eyes while back home my flu-ridden mother was snuggling happily, flipping the pages of a movie magazine.

"I've decided to go into business with you," Aunt Ruby told Dad, as if it were a done deal. "I could do with a good challenge, now that Frank's career is pretty much on automatic pilot."

"What do you know about the service station business?"

"Fast learner."

Dad laughed. "Speed of light."

"Then give me the chance and give yourself a new lease on life."

They haggled for the next half hour. There were things they'd probably never agree on, but it was becoming clear that my father was letting go of his total control.

"Better leave the mink at home, Ruby," he said. "Get yourself a pair of coveralls."

They had to be kidding. Aunt Ruby with gasoline dabbed behind her ears. It was a cartoon out of *Dogpatch* or *Major Hoople's Boarding House*. It was *My Mother the Car* with silk seats and a fur-trimmed steering wheel. But somehow the cares of the *blankety-blank* Texaco were dissolving in a puff of smoke right out of *I Dream of Jeannie*.

★

Some people have to scale the Himalayas to get attention. Or rob banks. Or sing like doves. Or take their clothes off and spread their naked selves across polar bear rugs. All I had to do was be a Tedley, son of a heart attack. When Monday rolled around, Math and History were nothing compared to my story. When Miss Luther finally grew tired of Dana Toad stage-whispering lines like "Did he fall to the floor?" and "Did the ambulance driver give him mouth to mouth?" she gave up on the French Revolution and offered me her spot at the head of the class. I described my father's heart attack as if it were an adventure saga, using my best *Twilight Zone* voice. I imagined the chills running up and down Marco's spine, the goose bumps blossoming on Wendy Fergie's arms.

"My Dad's will to live is as strong as LBJ's," I concluded. Miss Luther asked if anyone had a question. All twenty-five kids sat there looking down at their desks or staring over my shoulders. Miss Luther cleared her throat as she always did when she was about to scold us for making too much noise. She said there was something she'd like to ask.

"You haven't mentioned your mother," she said. "How's she doing? Is she spending most of her time at the hospital?"

For a moment, I thought Miss Luther had somehow heard about my mother refusing to accompany the ambulance on the night of the heart attack. But her question would be mean if she already knew the answer. No doubt she expected my mother to play a role in such a life-changing event. Ordinary families went through crises together. What would a normal mother have done and still be doing? What was the right lie to tell?

"She took a cab with us to the hospital," I said, keeping it simple. "But then she got the flu."

Miss Luther clearly expected more and might have asked me to elaborate, as when she was checking up on my studies, if a hand hadn't gone up across the room. Wendy Fergie's.

"Weren't you afraid that your father might die?"

Suddenly, everyone was looking at me. Fear was something they understood better than superhuman bravery. How could I explain that my mother owned all the fear in our family, and that my father's anger and his dismissal of weakness were far more powerful than a puny thing like death?

If I started talking about fear, I wasn't sure what might come out—a raven? A flash of lightning? I stood silent for what felt like the rest of my life until Miss Luther clapped her hands and drew us back to French history again.

THREE

WITHOUT DAD, the Texaco station was glittering in the noon hour sun, business booming, tools clanging, gas gurgling. The one and only Frankie Wilde was manning the gas pumps, wearing the cleanest pair of white coveralls I'd ever seen. He had a two-fingered grip on the gas nozzle, like Billy the Kid clutching his gun. And while he washed and wiped windshields, he was humming something by The Statler Brothers. Inside the garage, Neil, the cool mechanic, stood beneath the undercarriage of a silver-grey Cadillac, his wrench flashing like a dagger. But most impressive of all was Aunt Ruby, swivelling in Dad's chair in the main office, handling the telephone like a pro, breezing through invoices and guzzling Coke. She was wearing tight black pants and a short grey jacket with black collar and cuffs. Her shiny black hair was piled high.

I didn't stick around for long. Uncle Frank gave me a gas nozzle salute, Neil tipped his wrench in my direction.

Aunt Ruby glowed. "Look at me, sweetie pie, I'm learning the ropes."

★

On the morning Dad was discharged, Miss Luther let me go home early so I could be there when he arrived. When Aunt Ruby's car spun into the driveway, Dad's face looking eagerly out of the passenger window, I cried, "He's here."

Sloppy as a Saint Bernard, Lissy almost knocked him over. I gave him a sort of hug: a hip bump with one arm tossed over his shoulder.

"Oh, Ed," Mom gushed, holding her lips to his for at least ten seconds. She had dressed in her best skirt and sweater combo. Her shoulder-length hair swung. She couldn't keep her hands off him, went so far as to unbutton his shirt and fiddle with the hair on his chest. Even Aunt Ruby's glamour paled next to my mother's heat. My parents were occasionally affectionate toward one another, but never so racy.

One minute, emergency, kissfest the next. There was a bothersome buzzing deep inside my head. I hadn't planned on saying anything to Dad about Mom's behaviour while he was in the hospital, but after he'd settled in and we were sitting in the living room, drapes closed, Lissy colouring at the coffee table, still in her pajamas, Mom and Grammie in the kitchen, I said, "It's great you're home and all, and that Aunt Ruby is helping you not to worry about the Texaco, but what are we going to do about Mom?" I told him how I'd dressed her in layers for the taxi ride. "No way she would have been able to go if I hadn't made her."

"Jesus, Robby," he sighed, looking at me as if I were a cracked window or a blown fuse, something he was going to have to fix. "Your mother's a little high-strung, so what? Wait until you grow up and have a family. Lots of days you won't even want to get out of bed, let alone go outside." He reached over and patted me on my knee. "She manages to do the grocery shopping and the banking. She must have her good days."

"I went to the bank for her this month," I explained. It had made me feel grown up to be trusted with cheques and cash. I'd bought stamps for her just after New Year's and had picked up a bunch of things from the pharmacy on Kingston Road.

"You haven't gone grocery shopping for her yet. She can still manage the big stuff," he said. "Let up on it a little, will you, Robby? We'll figure out a way to get everything back to normal." He leaned forward. "Maybe it's a phase. You've heard of the change women go through. Maybe it's a temporary thing." I should have asked more of the questions that needed answers, like what about visiting Aunt Ruby and Aunt Veronica, or next year's Christmas shopping, or summer vacation.

Things did seem to improve over the next few days. No more than a peep about the Texaco when Aunt Ruby and Uncle Frank popped by to deliver a load of groceries. Everything was out of our hands there, out of our hands and under control.

One day after school, Dad, Mom and I played marathon Monopoly, strutting across Boardwalk, giggling at Community Chest cards, shrugging out of jail with an easy fifty bucks. One day we watched home movies. My parents were looking incredibly young. Lissy and I stumbled in and out of focus like a couple of windup ducks.

"Your moustache was sassy back then," Mom cooed, and Dad said, "You always knew how many buttons to leave undone. You could always guarantee a second look."

One night it was pancakes, followed by poetry. Mom recited Robby Burns in a terrible Scottish brogue. Dad offered Robert Service with a flourish:

> *I wanted the gold, and I sought it;*
> *I scrabbled and mucked like a slave.*
> *Was it famine or scurvy—I fought it;*
> *I hurled my youth into a grave.*

When we were too tired for more, Mom made caramel corn, which we devoured in a frenzy of sticky fingers. Even Queen Mary got a few kernels.

"A lovely evening," Mom said sleepily.

Nightly we joined Mom at the front window to see the world beyond the glass. No matter how much I'd been enjoying myself, looking out the window reminded me that board games and popcorn and poetry were diversions, that we were part of my mother's lockdown, pretending that everything we could possibly need was under this roof. Grammie Gorman always looked for robbers, drunks or other fishy characters, mumbling things like "Criminals don't even go to work until we're fast asleep" and "The suburbs are such easy pickings." Big game for Lissy was anything with four legs and a tail. Dad observed cars parked neatly in their driveways, while Mom preferred the emptiness of the street itself. Nothing more to think about, everything in its place.

"What about you?" Dad asked one night. "Would you like to be the man in the moon?"

"That would be incredibly lonely," I said.

"Maybe the earth looks lonely to the man in the moon," Mom said.

"Aren't the Russians colonizing the moon?" Grammie said. "You wouldn't be alone for long."

"A couple of cosmonauts wouldn't be much company," I said.

"You know what I think would be enough?" Dad said. "To be the moon and know that everyone on earth was watching you."

Mom shivered and let the curtains fall back.

*

Dad started calling his heart attack "a second chance." Sometimes at school I could think of nothing except the fun I was missing at home. At other times I was worried sick. Except for a few Wendy Fergie tingles and the occasional LBJ tidbit, my mind rarely left Arizona Avenue.

"Hey, let's check out old Franny and Lucy," Marco suggested one Friday afternoon. He gave me the kind of stage wink that made me wish I could laugh off my family and prowl the streets with him. But I said, "I've got to get home and be with my Dad. I'm helping him recuperate."

Truth was, he was recuperating perfectly well without me. When I got home that day, I found my parents in the bathroom. Lissy was sitting in the dry bathtub, slapping her hands against the porcelain. Dad was washing my mother's hair for her, the two of them bent over the bathroom sink, his hands all fluffy pink suds.

"Are you in for a dandy of a surprise," he said, grinning himself silly. "A new woman in your life."

Grammie Gorman groaned from out in the living room. "There are limits to love, Ed Tedley," she shouted.

I was with Grammie when my new mother appeared.

"Platinum blonde," she explained, her lips bright, her skin creamy.

"I've always wanted to snuggle up to a blonde," Dad said.

"Now I'm his fantasy as well as his wife."

"Now you're my blonde bombshell. Jean Harlow and Marilyn Monroe all rolled up into one Flo Tedley."

Lissy cried when she saw the blonde hair. Mom had to whisper the kind of sweet nothings that helped her go to bed each night. Queen Mary hightailed it into the basement and Grammie simply shut her eyes, complaining of glare. I didn't know what to say. Was this "new mother" a fake, or was her fear being temporarily disguised? Her eyes still had those big pupils, as if she were seeing ghosts. But I didn't have to say anything. Dad did enough gushing for the both of us.

*

Dad asked me to accompany him on his first expedition since his heart attack. He was going to check out how everything was faring at the Texaco. He promised Mom that he'd keep his adrenalin on low. I was proud to be out on the Scarborough streets with him, like he was one of those war heroes waving from convertibles in Remembrance Day parades.

"God, it feels like I've just shucked my cocoon," he said, inhaling the mild, late-afternoon air.

No more than ten footsteps into our stroll, his pace quickened to something brisk and devil-may-care. He was eyeing everything with a smile, from baby carriages to spaniels, from the litter of last fall's leaves to noisy little kids playing road hockey, nodding whenever he passed another walker.

"Let me tell you something, Robby," he said. "Fresh air beats everything, booze, caffeine, whatever. I can feel the kick." He took a deep breath. "I've always hated being cooped up. My lungs feel like they're collapsing when there's not enough room to breathe."

"You like our house though, don't you?"

He laughed. "Sure I do, but even heaven would become stale if you were stuck on a cloud day in and day out."

My mind couldn't fit him on a cloud. I could easily imagine Mom sunk to her waist in a cotton ball, comfortable with that kind of soft enclosure. "I guess it all depends on what your house is like," I suggested. "You never know what you're going to find at our place."

"Do you realize how many choices there are, Robby?" he asked, his eyes shining. "Too many to waste my days with socket wrenches and gaskets."

He was off on a completely different tangent, into some convoluted plan about taking a long walk every day until he'd walked around the entire planet, a new, slightly loopy version of himself. Were both my parents insisting on becoming other people? Was I going to have to come up with a new identity as well?

We arrived at the Texaco a little out of breath. It looked suspiciously quiet, but the minute we rounded the corner into the front lot, the garage doors were flung open and more than two dozen regular customers burst out in a chorus of "For he's a jolly good fellow." Aunt Ruby had strung crepe paper across the window and there was a hand-lettered bristol board sign that read, WELCOME BACK, HEART & SOUL OF TEDLEY'S TEXACO.

A single red rose leaned over the rim of a coffee cup on the neatly ordered office desk. The peanut machine was full. Cans of motor oil were stacked in a pyramid, the shelf of road maps arranged in order of province and city.

"Speech! Speech!"

"Take it away, Ed!" Aunt Ruby roared.

Dad stood with his back to the festive office window, looking out on the assembled crowd of loyal customers, the sparkling gas pumps, the traffic on Kingston Road. At first I thought he might be basking in the attention. I imagined his heart pounding with joy. But I soon began to sense a wariness, a withering of his energies. No way was he going to let them sweep him off his feet.

"Flattery will get you everywhere," he finally said, "but I'll be damned if I'm spending one more second underneath your rusty cars."

Everyone roared approval and burst into applause. Ed Tedley and his new attitude were a hit. After twenty minutes of making nice, he was drained. He didn't need any coaxing to leave. He raised his right arm into the air—thank you and that's enough for now—and turned away from all the bustle. He headed home at a slower pace, quiet as he walked, weary, me beside him, invisible.

*

During the Easter break, Marco and I had part-time jobs at Tedley Texaco. Our duties were to do everything we could before Dad had a chance to, freeing him to sit at his desk and feel healthy and in control again. Aunt Ruby had been such a wizard with the books that on her days off the money end of things was easy to keep track of. The station was now so efficient that Dad's anxiety skimmed over the surface of days like a flat stone.

My duties felt endless. The job made me realize I wanted to do something with my life requiring more brains than brawn. Pumping gas (careful not to dribble), always with a smile and a "Thank you, sir" or "ma'am," washing windshields (careful not to smudge or stare), adding oil (careful not to spill), installing fan belts and hefting batteries, fetching screwdrivers and cables, nuts and wires, making change, making small talk. Marco spent most of his shifts in the garage with Neil, handing him one tool or another. We both agreed that no matter what the task, the hardest part was the constant striving to please someone.

"The customer is always right," Dad explained. "They can never be too happy."

We served, scooted, smiled, we leapt and crawled, acting as if everyone's slightest wish was our greatest pleasure. "This'll make men out of you," several of the customers said, meaning that we'd be completely tired out by the end of a shift.

By the night of the third day, I was too worn down after work to do anything but flop. It was the most exhausted I'd ever been. After she slid a pan of brownies into the oven, Mom offered me the mixing bowl to lick and I said no thanks. I'd never refused that before. I couldn't even prop up enough cards to play gin rummy with Dad.

Exhaustion divided me from everything, from episodes of *Hawk* and *Family Affair*, from hanging out with Louie Burr and Dana Toad. When Dad told me about the Russian space probe crashing into Venus, I didn't even have the get-up-and-go to imagine the fireball. Exhaustion had made the world seem smaller.

Mid-way through my fifth day of pumping gas and being perfect, just when I thought I was going to drop, Uncle Frank appeared. "Hey, glum face," he said, "how about a little country sunshine?" His guitar was slung over his shoulder and he was wearing a white cowboy hat. After a few strums, my father emerged from the office. A few more, and Neil and Marco poked their heads out of the garage, both of them black-faced. Uncle Frank broke into loud song, his "Easter Treat," right there beside the pumps, in full view of Kingston Road. He sang every bit as loud as the traffic, a megaphone of country and western, sunlight bouncing off his white hat.

Before long the place was packed with all makes of cars with engines shut off, windows rolled down, destinations abandoned. The sidewalk beyond the station filled up with dog walkers, groups of kids and women pushing baby carriages. Tedley's Texaco had been transformed into a Nashville honky-tonk. Uncle Frank dug deep into his repertoire of Buck Owens, Eddy Arnold and Jim Reeves' greatest hits, finally reaching his own high note with "Tearjerker," complete with weepy voice breaks and yodelling after the closing chorus. The crowd loved it. After the last yodel, he sang the whole thing over again.

I leaned against a gas pump and looked out at all the smiles. Here and there were familiar faces: Mrs. Burr and Linda, Mr. Kraag, our geography teacher, and Lonny Milford, with his arm thrown around a pimply-faced redhead. When my eyes met Wendy Fergie's eyes, Uncle Frank was into the second round of yodelling. It didn't matter that my coveralls were filthy or that a long piece of my hair hung over my left eye, causing me to blink every five seconds. Wendy Fergie looked at me with a mixture of admiration and envy. I wasn't just her IQ equal, but an insider, member of a crowd-drawing family. At the end of the concert, while Uncle Frank took bows and signed autographs, Wendy headed straight over.

"How are you?" she asked politely.

"Mainly exhausted," I said, nervous enough to be truthful instead of cool. "How about you?"

"Fine, I guess. Except that my life seems so boring compared to yours."

"It does?"

"Who is that man?" she asked, pointing a little dreamily at Uncle Frank.

"My uncle."

I gathered every bit of cool I could manage. I liked what I saw of myself in Wendy's eyes. Returning to work, I brandished the gas nozzle with the panache of a juggler until I was sure she was out of sight, then stuck it into the slot, thinking it isn't easy, being a man.

Dad rolled me out of bed at seven thirty the next morning, hustling me through my breakfast and shower. Two hours later we were standing in the middle of Eaton's downtown, wondering what to buy my mother for her birthday.

"How about one of those gold-coloured scarves?" I suggested, thinking how it would match her new hair. "Or some French perfume, or fancy slippers."

"Clear away all those cobwebs," Dad said. "I'm fed up with clichés."

We looked at a Jayne Mansfield-like leopard print dress, a fire engine red negligee with matching feather boa and a set of rhinestone earrings that dangled like chandeliers. We left a trail of blushing sales ladies behind us. Each time he rejected some item, Dad became more self-assured and also more bizarre.

"What has she always secretly wanted?" he asked a tight-lipped mannequin.

"A book of poetry?" I asked. "A knife sharpener?" These seemed a little on the daring side.

"I've got it!" he shouted, clicking his heels and heading for the nearest escalator. Just when I thought he might be running in circles, he turned left on the fourth floor, bypassed the pianos and headed for a sales desk in the midst of woodwinds and piccolos and such.

"Perfect," he said. "Absolutely perfect. I should have thought of this years ago."

"A clarinet?"

"No, sir. An accordion. And I want the best."

The best turned out to be a thirty-pound black and silver Caruso, half-piano, half-iron lung, which came nestled in a satin-lined case.

"Are you sure?" I said as the clerk rang up the bill. "Accordions aren't good for much more than polkas."

"Your mother loves the accordion," he insisted. "Her Uncle

Russ played one at our wedding. A great rendition of "The Anniversary Waltz."" He got a hazy look in his eyes. "She said it sounded like every instrument in the world rolled into one."

"But she can't play."

"So, it's a gift that will continue for the whole year. She'll take lessons and serenade us under the crabapple."

There he went again, putting Mom in an impossible situation. I couldn't see it. She and the crabapple tree lived in completely separate worlds, even though only a thin sheet of glass separated them. I thought the accordion might scare her. It sometimes gasped like Dad did back in February, the night of his attack.

As he was unable to carry the accordion on account of his bad heart, I had to be the muscle man, stumbling through Eaton's with a thirty-pound beast banging against my shins.

★

The last day of work was horrible, windy with raindrops the size of ball bearings. I was pinned to the gas pumps by a steady stream of headlights, drenched sweater and jeans beneath my raincoat like another layer of skin. I squelched the whole way home. But neither parent even noticed me dripping in the hall as I removed my saturated shoes.

"Come on," Dad called. "We've got forty-four years of gorgeousness to celebrate."

"If you say my age one more time, Ed Tedley, I'll wring your neck."

"Okay," said Dad when I entered the living room, clapping his hands together, "now that Robby's here, let the party begin. First stop, the greatest dinner of them all. Luigi's Italian Eatery, a little Sicily in Scarborough, spaghetti that melts in your mouth."

"Smaghetti," Lissy crooned.

"Linguine, tortellini, macaroni, spumoni, hey, Brio," my father sang. Was he pretending to forget that the birthday girl couldn't leave the house? Did a trick like that stand a chance?

"Let's dazzle the Italians with your blonde birthday curls."

"I'd rather order in," Mom said. It was ages since we'd been to Luigi's. In fact it might have been last year's birthday, back in the days when she was capable of walking through the front door. Did Dad think he could fast-talk her into changing back into the woman she used to be?

I couldn't stand the tension. "Yeah, let's order in," I said. Helping her stay home would be my birthday gift. I couldn't bear to bundle her up again. I didn't want to walk into the restaurant with the Michelin Man.

"Luigi's is too dark anyway, you can't see what you're putting in your mouth."

"Dark is romantic, you silly goose. Dark is atmosphere."

"We'll light candles here," I insisted, "and play Frank Sinatra records."

"Sounds very romantic to me," Mom agreed.

I think Dad would have gone for this if not for Grammie's world-famous selfishness. I'm sure she knew what she was doing, pushing us into a showdown.

"I'd like a night out myself," she said.

"It's settled then," my father said.

If he'd dashed out on his own to warm up the car, Mom might have had time to concoct a sudden headache. If he'd paused for even ten seconds, she might have been able to dream up another reason for not going to Luigi's—too loud, too smelly. If Grammie hadn't immediately gone hard at my cowlick, I might have come up with the perfect ruse: "Didn't Lissy throw up the last time we ate out?"

But there wasn't time for even a measly *but*. Dad playfully grabbed Mom's hand and started tugging her toward the door. She slid a few feet across the carpet. When it seemed she might continue sliding right out into the damp and dismal night, she stopped resisting and sat down in the middle of the living room. I could see the veins bulging in Dad's arms as he held on to her. Lissy knelt down next to Mom and whimpered. Dad gave another tug and now he was dragging Mom across the carpet, which is when she opened her mouth and let loose a high-pitched scream that I will never forget. She held it to the very end of her breath. Grammie took a few steps back into the dining room, shocked. Lissy's whimper rose to a moan.

"Jesus Murphy," Dad said, letting go of Mom's arm. The scream stopped as suddenly as it had begun. She rose to her feet and brushed the wrinkles from her skirt. Nothing more needed to be said. I walked over to the dining room and rummaged around in one of the china cabinet drawers until I found Luigi's takeout menu.

Once the food arrived, we ate quietly, tension easing with each bite. The scream had cleared the air, put us back in touch with the way things were. Dad recovered his party mood. After Grammie had cleared the table, he made Mom close her eyes and count to twenty. When she opened them again, the silver and black accordion was shining up at her from its blue satin box.

"But I can't play," she said, exactly as I had predicted.

"You'll learn," Dad promised, "and next year this time you'll be playing at Luigi's."

Mom made a small o with her lips as if she might scream again, but she leaned down and stroked the silver grillwork then gently released the snap that held the bellows together. "I can probably play the keys a bit," she said, smiling. "I like how beautifully it sits in its case." She lifted the instrument from the floor, balanced it on her thighs and let the bellows fall open, which released a strange, truncated cry.

On the ivories she played a bit of "Three Blind Mice."

FOUR

BEFORE HEADING OFF to the hairdresser one April morning, Grammie Gorman, who had been doing bits of grocery shopping, disagreed with so many things on Mom's shopping list that she refused to go until my mother came to her senses and made a more healthy list. When I arrived home for lunch at noon, Young's Fruit Market van was parked in our driveway.

"Just a few groceries," Mom explained as Mr. Young scurried back and forth from the van with bags full of Sugar Puffs, bread and butter pickles, rum and raisin ice cream, Vanilla Wafers, raisin bagels, lemonade, wieners and Spam. For the first time I realized that it might really be possible for a person to live the rest of her life at home without going outside.

Unfortunately for Mom, Dad arrived home early while Mr. Young was still unloading.

"What's wrong?" he asked, barging through the front door. "Why are the groceries being delivered?" People who had groceries delivered were old folks or crazy women who lived with a houseful of cats.

"Grammie was supposed to go, but she refused to buy any of the things you like. I can't see you living without your Spam and sweets."

"I could have done the shopping this time."

"I'd like to see that," she said, rolling her eyes. "You can't even run the gas station anymore without help from my sister."

"You want me to work night and day again? How about I drive around the city looking for another heart attack?"

"Better that than give me a nervous breakdown. This household is my responsibility and I don't appreciate criticism of things you can't begin to understand."

"Fine and dandy," he sputtered. "Why not order yourself a new husband next time you call the grocery store."

He stomped back outside and drove away in a burst of exhaust. Mom made her own flurry by tossing groceries into the cupboards, muttering. Was she trying to drive him away? Would she have felt safer if we all disappeared? People got divorced in the soaps, but the process usually took so long they often turned around and got remarried. Occasionally, without warning, a character would be played by a new actor. Might there be a different version of my father out there who never knew that once upon a time his wife used to leave the house?

*

Aunt Ruby dropped by the day after the fight.

"Mother told me about your little birthday episode," she said to Mom. She sat in the velour chair, across the room from my mother on the couch. I lurked in the hall.

"I can do what I want on my own birthday," she said.

"Have you ever thought of trusting us?" Aunt Ruby asked. "If you told us what you're afraid of, maybe we'd understand."

"How can I describe something that has no logic. The worst thing you can imagine, that's exactly what it's like." She looked up at the living room ceiling. "It feels like I'm going to die. I don't know how to describe it, Ruby. It started out with little things, like tripping on the bottom step of the front porch. Slipping on a patch of ice on the driveway. Then I started thinking about the sewers running underneath the street and the darkness behind the hedge. And the sky, how does it manage to stay up there without caving in and crushing us? It just got out of hand." She shrugged her shoulders. "I may have stayed inside too long. Too much housework, too many troubles with Lissy. Whole weeks went by when I'd never get any further than the front window. One day it hit me. I didn't have a choice anymore. I could hardly touch a doorknob without feeling faint."

Aunt Ruby was nothing if not plucky. She probably wasn't afraid of anything. "Let's go outside right this minute," she said, slapping her hands on her knees, rising to her feet. "Live or die."

Momentary excitement made my head feel untethered to my neck, but it disappeared the minute Aunt Ruby stood up. I began to feel queasy, completely unready. I backed down the hall, then further, into the kitchen, where I could hear everything. A chair creaked. Some footsteps. More footsteps. Silence. Then another creak from a chair, followed by the grinding sound of the storm door slowly opening. I could hear outdoor noises more clearly: a car whooshing by, kids squealing, an airplane passing overhead. I held my breath. I could almost feel the muscles stretching in Aunt Ruby's arms as she pulled Mom toward the front porch. Then a whole jumble of sounds: scrapes, a yelp, a scuffle, thumps. I heard the front door bang against the hall closet.

Finally, I heard Mom's voice as clear as a knock on my skull.

"See?" she said, victorious. "See what I mean? That almost killed me."

*

After Aunt Ruby left, I laid on my bed staring at the ceiling, wondering why people in novels find staring at the ceiling a good way to collect their thoughts. Both my father and Aunt Ruby had failed to force Mom physically out the front door. Were they simply not strong enough, treating her as if she were breakable? Was some weakness stopping them from going all the way? If it were me, I'd approach this like I do a tug of war, using just enough strength to hold on, waiting for her to tire herself out, then overwhelming her with a blast of energy at the last minute.

Those things she was afraid of, the sewers and the falling sky, why wasn't she afraid of the Vietnam War, or of people starving to death in India? Those were the sorts of things people were right to be afraid of. Would she be afraid of me if I insisted she sweep aside her fears? I pictured us standing side by side in the middle of Arizona Avenue, her shaking and crying but having to agree that the sky was still above her. Wouldn't Dad be proud of me? Grammie Gorman could go back to her apartment. The world could stop revolving around my mother's stubbornness and go back to being immense.

*

I was outside in the backyard a few days later, playing golf on the mini-course Dad and I had made with tin cans sunk in the grass the summer before. Every time I came close to my parent's bedroom window, I imagined, somewhere in the future, a tour guide pointing at it and announcing, "This is where Mrs. Tedley lived in fear for fifty years." I was at the far end of the yard, back in the bushes having hit my ball too far, when Mom stepped out onto the back porch.

Was I hallucinating? I stayed in the bushes and watched. How clumsy she looked, as if the porch were the edge of a cliff. She was wearing a thick pink sweater and had on one of Dad's baseball caps. She never lifted her eyes from her feet.

She froze several times. Then her entire upper body began to sway. She moved her feet apart, trying to keep her balance. She raised her arm to grasp at something like an invisible railing or rope. Several times it seemed she would fall flat on her face into the forsythia. She was shaking so badly her legs wouldn't move. She swayed, then stumbled. Finally, she let herself fall backward, grabbed the handle of the screen door and slowly dragged herself back inside. It was the saddest sight I'd ever seen, sadder than Lissy's drool, sadder than Dad's feet sticking out from under a car at the Texaco.

I arrived home from school the next day to find Diana Costello sitting on one end of our couch and Mom, hypnotized by the sad details of Diana's life, on the other. Diana had dropped by for no particular reason a few times, but I hadn't seen her up close for over a year. They were facing one another, knees curled up, almost touching. Nothing to be concerned about, I said to myself, sitting down in the chair beside the stereo. I flicked on CHUM-AM, low enough not to really bother them, but loud enough that Diana would have to turn up her own volume. Mom tossed me a half-hearted frown.

"What's the use of making friends," Diana complained, "when I can't invite them home? The drunker my mother gets, the more she likes to reminisce. She could talk the ear off a stalk of corn. And my father likes to pick fights, anything at all, taxes, religion, mashed potatoes versus french fries. Friends I invite over would have to be deaf, dumb and blind."

She was pale and ashy, like a cloud of cigarette smoke. I didn't like the way she made me feel and I didn't like her.

When B.J. Thomas came on the radio, singing "I'm So Lonesome I Could Cry," Diana Costello made a strange hiccupping sound, like she was trying to catch a sob before it got away.

"I love this song," she said.

I didn't want the song to be Diana's. This was my song. I'd already made up all sorts of alternate lines: *I'm so lonesome I could stand on my head and spit teardrops; I'm so lonesome I could water the lawn with my tears; I'm so lonesome you might as well call me Niagara Falls.*

Diana Costello's situation was much worse than mine. My parents weren't alcoholics. I had lots of friends. I could even get along with the Remington twins if I put my mind to it. But imagine

Marco, or Louie, or Wendy Fergie, standing beside the ninth hole of my father's mini-course, watching my mother stumble across the back porch like a zombie. Marco would hardly have had to embellish that story.

B.J. stopped singing and the mood changed. Diana Costello continued with her reasons for being the way she was, but now she seemed to be glowing. Did I glow sometimes too? What did people see when they looked at me? Relatives had remarked that I was like my mother—what did they mean? In a stranger's eyes would it be clear that my mother was pretty much always terrified? Was there a part of me that would one day fall apart?

*

I was slouched over my book in Miss Luther's class, wondering how one world could produce two women as different as Mrs. Gandhi and Mom, when Wendy Fergie breezed past my desk on her way to the bathroom and dropped a small pink envelope onto the page of my book.

Wendy was too bold to shut herself off from the outside world. If she got locked in a tower, she'd let her hair down like Rapunzel, and anyone who wanted to could climb up and join her.

Dear Robinson, The pleasure of your company is requested at my fourteenth birthday party, on Friday April 30th at 8 PM. I await your reply with high hopes.

*

Grammie Gorman's seventieth birthday was a stay-at-home celebration. No one even suggested eating out. Dinner, courtesy of Chopsticks Chinese Food Takeout, delivered to our door in a yellow Volkswagen bug with a pair of red and black chopsticks painted on the doors, consisted of egg rolls, steamed rice, chickie chow mein (as I used to call it when I was still a kid), vegetable chop suey, sweet and sour spareribs and fortune cookies. Aunt

Ruby and Uncle Frank brought a two-decker chocolate cake with seven white candles arranged in the shape of a zero, as if Grammie might be starting all over again. Aunt Veronica and Uncle Maurice supplied the drinks, including a homemade mixture of ginger ale and Welch's grape juice. Everything any family could need to make a successful celebration.

But the mood inside this little bomb shelter of a party was completely different from what we'd been experiencing lately. We were on our best behaviour. "Wait until I tell you…" Aunt Veronica must have said at least ten times, as if she were checking off a list of spellbinding stories, a few of them obviously someone else's, but borrowed to multiply the image of herself as the kind of person fascinating things were always happening to. "You'll never guess…"

Aunt Ruby competed for attention, launching into a wacky Texaco tale that made the service station sound like a Marx Brothers' movie.

The talk grew louder when Grammie started opening her presents. Aunt Ruby told a long, complicated tale of how she'd found the fancy red dress with silver buttons in a little hole-in-the-wall boutique on Avenue Road near Davenport. She snatched the dress from Grammie's hands and held it up against her own body, swishing from side to side. "Isn't it divine?" she asked no one and everyone. Grammie snatched it back, clutching it to her chest, warning Aunt Ruby that she was going to have to take her out to lunch so she could show it off.

Aunt Veronica's gift was a pale blue spring hat that everyone agreed would look wonderful in Edwards Gardens, a grand place for a picnic once spring was a little further along. Despite Grammie's lack of cooperation, Aunt Veronica managed to squash the hat onto her wiry curls. It made her look like one of Red Skelton's sad drunks. Cousin Roma followed with a guidebook to North American birds, which caused Grammie to roll her eyes and say, "If only I had the time to sit outside and count the birds." This took some of the pressure off my gift: a fake leopard skin back scratcher I'd bought at Woolworths with my own money.

"For those hard to reach places," Uncle Maurice said with an explosive guffaw that made Grammie glare at me. But before her mood could escalate into genuinely bad, Mom shoved her present onto Grammie's lap. Beneath neatly folded tissue paper in three shades of pink was a box containing a lilac-coloured summer nightgown with matching kimono.

"Beautiful!" Aunt Veronica exclaimed. "Where did you find it, Flo?"

Mom looked down at her lap as if the gift had left some trace of itself on her blue skirt. "The Eaton's catalogue," she said, her voice barely above a whisper.

"There are some lovely things in the catalogue," Aunt Ruby said.

"It's so tricky," Aunt Veronica piped up. "You can't feel the material in a catalogue."

Dad, never one to linger over other people's bad behaviour, announced second cups of coffee all around, and the stories started up again. Aunt Veronica repeated a rumour about the wife of Scarborough's mayor fooling around with her optometrist. Then there was Aunt Ruby's nightlife calendar. The service station may have slowed her down a bit, but she and Uncle Frank still made the rounds, doing all sorts of crazy things, like the Twist at some nightclub in the west end after drinking three Bloody Marys each. Even Dad got a big laugh describing how at a recent appointment his heart specialist's nurse had walked in on him before he'd had a chance to put on his paper gown.

At one point I heard Mom mention Diana Costello's name, but neither Aunt Ruby nor Aunt Veronica were much interested in the sad plight of an alcoholic family and quickly changed the subject. So when I saw Mom disappear into her bedroom, I thought she'd gone for the night, until I heard Uncle Frank's voice rising above the others.

"What have we got here? Looks like Flo's in charge of the entertainment."

Mom was standing in the doorway, stooped under the weight

of her accordion, swaying a little. "I've been practicing every morning. I thought you might like to hear."

She didn't bother with an introduction, but launched into "Row, Row, Row Your Boat, " followed by "Pop Goes the Weasel" and finally "Rock-a-Bye Baby." When she finished Dad called for an encore and she played each song through again. It was as if she had suddenly turned into a seven-year-old at a recital.

The next afternoon, trying to recover from the previous day's snob-story competition, I was about to settle into a *Wild Kingdom* show about chimpanzees with Lissy when Dad joined us in the rec room, bursting with something to say.

"Speaking of wild animals, how would you like to spend some time with skunks and raccoons, maybe even a few of those soft-eyed deer that can break your heart with just one look?"

Lissy went nuts. "Now, now," she cried, pawing at Dad as if his pockets were full of furry beasts.

"Sure," I said, intrigued but cautious, thinking about wolves and bears, the kind of animals that might not be so welcoming.

"Okeydoke," he said happily, ready to let the whole thing spill out. "I'm thinking of buying some property, a cottage lot on the edge of this great little bay. Not too wild, mind you, but enough roughing it to make you feel like you're a thousand miles away."

"How?" I asked, as the list of impossibilities flooded in.

"Well, your Aunt Ruby knows a guy who wants to sell, and it's pretty cheap, considering it's only two hours from the city."

"But how?" I needed more details, more evidence that wiser minds had already cleared a path through Mom's problems.

"What do you mean, how? I'll write a cheque. We'll drive up on weekends. Eventually we'll build a cottage." He was more than a little bugged by my hesitation. He wanted a cheerleader like Lissy.

"But what about Mom?" I asked, zeroing in on the source of my discomfort. I wasn't sure I could handle adding to the list of places she couldn't go to.

"Ah," he said, like a safecracker listening to the spin and click of tumblers turning in a lock. "I've got that one figured out."

Lowering his voice, he explained. "She's too wrapped up in herself. She needs to start thinking about the rest of us, about how good the country will be for you and Lissy."

"Snakes," I said. "Bats. Poison ivy." I couldn't stand his simple-mindedness.

"Fiddlesticks," he said. "You wait and see. She'll forget all about herself when she sees Lissy chasing a hummingbird or you learning how to dive."

"How are you going to get her in the car?" I asked.

"Honest to Pete, Robby, you can be a real killjoy."

I thought this over for a minute. "Maybe we could put curtains on the back and side windows," I suggested.

His whole face burst into a smile. He rose to his feet, his head brushing the rec room ceiling.

"Perfect. We'll turn the back seat into a hideaway. She won't even know she's left home."

★

While getting ready for Wendy Fergie's birthday party the following Friday, I tried to picture Wendy and me holding hands, or kissing, but that was as far as I could get without my legs starting to shake a little. It wasn't so much what to do that perplexed me, but what to say before and after doing it. I contemplated asking Mom whether she might have any advice. But when I came out of my bedroom, expecting a compliment about how good I looked with my hair slicked back and my Sunday shoes shined, she said, "I don't think you should go." Dad was still at the Texaco and Grammie had gone back to her apartment for one night.

"What if something happens?"

"Dad will be home before nine," I said. "And there's always the phone."

She nodded, but it was plain to see that her discomfort went deeper than clocks and phones. She seemed to be barely listening to my reassurances. "It's just a feeling," she said. "I wish you

64

wouldn't go."

I tried to picture Wendy Fergie's party without me, but blanked.

"This is important to me," I said. "I have to go."

Her cheeks caved in a little. I wondered how I'd feel if something terrible did happen, but not going to the party would feel like throwing gasoline on a fire in order to put it out.

Still, I felt guilty about leaving, though meeting up with Marco at the corner helped distract me. He launched into one of his gross sex talks, giving me other things to worry about.

"You've got to remember to not let your pubic hairs get stuck together while you're doing it. That could really hurt when you try to separate them afterwards. And you have to make sure you don't keep a boner too long. You can do permanent damage to your balls. But you can't go too fast either. Girls like to be fingered for a while. You should always carry lots of Kleenex in your pockets in case you come all over her dress."

The distance between an XO at the bottom of a pink party invitation and me shooting all over Wendy Fergie's dress was impossible to cross.

"For Christ's sake, will you shut the fuck up," I snapped. That startled him into silence.

By the time we arrived at the party, I felt dirty and unsafe. My eyes burned in their sockets, and I kept getting semi-erections for no reason at all. Wendy looked like sherbet in a raspberry-coloured dress with a white lace collar. I didn't dare go near her.

It took two good hours of eating chips, drinking Cokes and listening to Elvis Presley, Johnny Rivers and Ronnie Dove records before I could relax enough to let the music into my body. With the lights turned down and The Righteous Brothers breaking into "Soul and Inspiration," I finally got up the nerve to dance with Wendy. But I was so obsessed with keeping a space between our bodies below the waist that the dance felt more like teetering on the edge of the Grand Canyon than anything resembling sex.

"It's okay," Wendy whispered, her breath filling my ear. I didn't have a clue what she meant: boners, my mother's fears, the Vietnam War. The heat of her body caused my shoulders to soften to a slump. Leaning into her, I could feel parts of my body connecting with hers, belly to belly, thigh against thigh. I could feel the shape of her small breasts as they spread out a little across my ribs. It was like I was falling into her in slow motion, every nerve sizzling, every pore sparking.

FIVE

DAD WAS UP WITH THE SUN on Saturday morning, waking me from a dream where I was holding one of Wendy Fergie's feet in my lap, trying to get her toes to wiggle.

"Come on, we're going to the bush."

He and Uncle Frank had already had their coffee and were raring to go, both of them bundled in ratty sweaters. Lissy was still asleep but Grammie had made plans for the two of them to take the streetcar downtown later in the day, just for the ride.

"Don't bother coming home until you've got this whole idea out of your system," Mom said. Dad laughed. He said he'd take pictures.

The trip was smooth all the way. Dad and Uncle Frank listened to country music, singing along, no matter how corny the tune. I read road signs and watched for wild animals. Pickering, Whitby, Oshawa, Bowmanville. Highways 401 to 115 to 7 to Side Road Number Ten. More cows than people. Peterborough, Norwood, Havelock. Two hours and six minutes after leaving Arizona Avenue, we were bumping along a dirt road past an old dog and two white horses grazing in a wide, rocky field. The sign for Grey Bay was a homemade job with a crooked red arrow that I suppose was meant to point straight ahead. Fields turned into swamps, which eventually turned into forest. I saw small, multicoloured cabins, weather-beaten outhouses, wooden swings hanging from tree branches and several canoes overturned in long grasses.

"Welcome to paradise," Dad said, coming to a stop at the end of the road.

In my imagination, a lot was something flat and bare and ready for a cottage. But this piece of land was wilderness with walls of trees and massive boulders. Vines, fallen branches, mud. The beach was at the bottom of a steep hill, also rocky and bushy.

The water of the actual bay was spooky silver, like the dull side of tinfoil. The bottom dropped off deep a few feet from shore. There was so much seaweed it was like looking through drowned men's beards. The whole thing gave me a squishy feeling in the pit of my stomach. It wasn't like me to be squeamish, but I was seeing partly from my mother's point of view. So much to be leery of: rotting leaves, slimy rocks, tangles, shadows. Walking along the top of the hill, I passed a garter snake, a pile of what could have been bear shit, a mess of puffballs that looked like brains and a freaky grey spider the size of a tablespoon. There were no people to spy on, no telephone lines to connect us to the rest of the world. Without electricity, how could we watch *The Secret Storm*? Our toilet was to be nothing more than a hole in the ground.

Dad couldn't have cared less what anyone thought. He was too busy dashing back and forth from the beach to the road, pointing out flat spots and twisted clumps of sumac, announcing "Tool shed!" or "Pump house!" At one point he leapt on top of a half-rotten log and shouted, "A picture window right here!" He wasn't talking to me.

When Uncle Frank and Dad put their heads together, I knew it didn't matter what I felt. Soon we'd be travelling two hours and six minutes every weekend, whether I liked it or not. Maybe Mom would come with us, sealed into the back seat. Maybe she'd simply refuse, and spend Saturdays and Sundays at the living room window while Grammie and Lissy rode the streetcars and Dad and I cleared the wilderness.

Marco and I ended up in the Remington twins's backyard on Monday after school. Louie Burr climbed over his fence to join us, half-dragging, half-lifting Barfy behind him. We weren't doing much of anything, hanging around making small talk with the twins under their weeping willow, a tree with branches so long it created a shelter even without its full allotment of summer leaves.

"I bet Lonny Milford's screwed a dozen girls here," Marco said, kicking at a brown patch of stubby spring grass. Barfy immediately lunged for Marco's toe, snarling.

"Shhh," Louie hissed, cocking his head toward the ramshackle fence dividing the Remingtons' yard from the Milfords'. "You never know."

Franny, distracted by Barfy, said, "You never know what?"

A mischievous look crept over Marco's face. "You never know how small a cock could be until you pull down Louie's pants," he answered.

Fighting off a case of the giggles, Lucy joined in. "You never know how fast a cock can grow until you pull down Marco's pants."

"How about this?" I said. "You never know how fast three cocks can grow until you pull down Franny and Lucy's pants."

There was no telling where this might have led had Barfy not suddenly started barking, with the hairs on his back standing on end.

"Jesus Christ," Marco said. My breathing stopped cold. It was Diana Costello, standing a mere ten feet away, fixing her weird stare at some mysterious spot between my eyebrows and my eyeballs. "Your mother needs you right away," she announced.

I wished I could think of something cool and dismissive to say, but my tongue had turned into a blackboard eraser. As I walked away, the heat from Lucy and Franny was burning the back of my neck. I imagined Marco's brain trying to figure it out, whirring like the adding machine at the Texaco. I walked through my own front door as if entering *The Outer Limits*. Mom and Grammie were in the spare bedroom. Grammie was hurling clothes into an open suitcase while Mom hurled them out again. The floor was heaped with sweaters, stockings and flowered dresses. The minute they saw me, they both began to shout.

"I won't put up with it," Grammie yelled. "Don't ever let anyone blame you for their problems. Do you hear me, Robinson? Whatever you are is your own fault."

Mom looked more afraid than angry, although her voice still packed a wallop.

"Where else do we learn about life if not from our mothers?"

"And what are you teaching your own son?" Grammie asked. "To be afraid of everything." She started in on the packing again, not even bothering to fold her clothes.

"I didn't say you were the cause of my problems," Mom insisted. "I'm the sum of all the influences in my life. You're all a little bit responsible for me."

"Stop it." Grammie slammed the suitcase lid, some of her clothes still on the floor. "I raised my girls to tackle the world with their bare hands, with courage and independence all the way. It's you who've let me down."

"Please." Mom tried to wrestle the suitcase out of Grammie's hands, but she was either too weak or too afraid to really fight.

"Out of my way, Robinson."

Grammie stood in front of me, glaring, as if I actually had plans to block her escape. How could I have made a difference? Throw her to the ground, tie her up with her own clothes and lock her in a closet? I understood why she wanted out. She was feeling trapped, same as we all were.

"I'm not standing in your way," I said.

"Robby!" Mom cried as if she were acting out a scene from *Mutiny on the Bounty*.

"Leave the boy alone," Grammie said. "This is free will, Florence. If you want me back, you come for me yourself."

I followed Grammie to the front door, brushing past Diana, who was standing in the living room, looking useless. A cab was waiting in the driveway. The driver rushed halfway up the front porch to help Grammie with her suitcases.

"You know where my apartment is," I heard her say, unsure whether she was talking to me or to the cabbie. Grammie didn't like to ride in cabs. She preferred buses. But nothing could stand in her way once her mind was made up, not even herself.

When the cab pulled away, I left the house, crossed the street and headed down the Remingtons' driveway, into their backyard. Marco, Louie and the twins didn't appear to be playing You Never Know anymore. Louie was picking bits of willow bark from the tree. I took a huge, death-defying breath.

"Here's one for you," I said. "You never know how far a cock will go until you've followed Diana Costello."

A second or two of silence, then Marco gave a huge chortle. I was back. I was safe. I'd left both Diana and my mother behind in one clever line. This had to be what a double agent felt like every time he crossed to the other side.

★

I don't know what Mom told Dad about Grammie's sudden departure. The subject wasn't discussed in front of me. But Grammie's absence did something to my mother's entire body chemistry. Her skin turned a different shade of white, like eggshell. When she showed fear, her platinum blonde hair glowed eerily and the light in her dark brown eyes fizzled out. She seemed breakable. Even more unsettling, she stopped opening the living room drapes in the morning. The Milfords, Remingtons, Burrs and Costellos were erased from her universe.

I avoided going home until I was sure Dad would be back from work. Sometimes I hung around the swings and slides in the schoolyard for an hour and a half, kicking up dust with Marco and whoever else happened to have nothing better to do. I'd saunter home afterwards, no rush. One day I discovered Dad riding my bike one-handed, back and forth in front of our place, as if he'd stumbled into some time warp and was a kid again.

"Hey, Robby!" He waved with his free hand, pedalling to meet me. "What a beaut. It rides like a dream."

"What are you doing?"

"Just cruising up and down the street," he said. His hair had blown up away from his forehead. "Enjoying the light."

I looked past him to the living room window. The drapes were closed. We had definitely moved to another stage. So the two of us took turns riding in circles, doing wheelies for a while. Close to home, but not quite there.

*

The next day, Aunt Ruby's car was parked in the driveway and the living room drapes and sheers were flung open, window glass shining like a sheet of fire.

"Aunt Ruby, Aunt Ruby!"

I burst through the back door, actually happy to be home. I ran my fingers along the edge of the sink, the backs of the kitchen chairs, the doorknobs, feeling how every surface was smooth and polished. Aunt Ruby wasn't alone in the living room. Lissy was there, cross-legged in a corner, dressing and undressing half a dozen Barbies. A stranger was in the room as well, a small, red-haired man, sitting straight as a parrot on a perch. He had a waxy-looking moustache and tiny wire glasses, the kind Grammie called spectacles.

"This is my nephew," Aunt Ruby said, and the red-haired man nodded in my direction without actually looking at me. He was giving all of his attention to Mom, who was fidgeting in one of our easy chairs. The accordion was sitting on the rug beside her. She seemed terribly uneasy, and kept nervously licking her lips.

"Just a few more questions, Mrs. Tedley," he said in a soft Scottish accent. "How well do you sleep?"

"Like a bug in a rug." One of her arms dangled over the side of the chair, her fingers stroking the top of the accordion.

"I see," he said, nodding, his eyebrows bunched in a frown. "And appetite?"

"Most days I could eat a horse." She was pawing the accordion now, making little thumping sounds with her knuckles.

"Good physical health is a blessing," he continued. "Now how about we try a little game? I'm going to give you a hypothetical situation and you tell me what it makes you feel. Here we go. I want you to imagine that your house has caught fire. The flames burn their way through the kitchen, into the dining room, the bedrooms, and are about to engulf the living room as well. You only have a minute or two to figure out what you're going to do."

I stood there, watching Mom tremble. Her eyes filled with tears. She did exactly what she'd do if a real fire ignited: sat, paralyzed, and wept.

"Be calm, Mrs. Tedley. Remember, this is just a hypothetical situation."

"It's only make-believe, Flo," Aunt Ruby reassured.

But Mom was beyond reassuring, lost within, slowly burning to a crisp. A hypothetical inferno was a pretty cruel thing to lay on someone.

Finally Aunt Ruby sank to her knees on the rug in front of Mom's chair, took Mom's stocking feet in both hands and massaged them, repeating over and over that everything was all right. The red-haired stranger stood and lifted one of Mom's wrists between his fingers, searching for her pulse. Slowly she came around. I fetched a cold washcloth and a glass of apple juice.

"I think that's enough for today," the man said, after Mom had taken a few sips of the juice.

"We call it 'agoraphobia,' translated from the Greek: fear of the marketplace. Fear of open spaces, as it were, recently classified as a Phobic Anxiety Disorder."

"I've got an agora sweater, Dr. McCurl," Aunt Ruby joked to lighten the mood. "Hopefully that doesn't mean that the sheep were scared out of their wits."

"That's angora," he corrected, stressing the 'n.'

"Phobic," my mother said, shuddering a little. "What a horrid word."

Dr. McCurl crouched down beside her chair. "It just means an extreme fear, Mrs. Tedley."

"Isn't there anything she can take to help with her nerves?" Aunt Ruby asked.

"There are several possibilities in the benzodiazepine family," he explained, "but we'll only resort to that if other treatments don't work."

"What other treatments?" I asked. I wasn't sure what to think of a doctor who terrified his patients with tales of their houses burning down. Was it hope or worry pinching my chest?

"I think we've had enough big words for one day," he said.

Aunt Ruby seemed comforted. "Dr. McCurl's a gem. We don't need to worry about a thing now. You know Lana Lake," she continued, "the one they call the Songbird of the North? You've heard her on *The Tommy Hunter Show*, the woman with the husky voice who sings Patsy Cline songs? Dr. McCurl cured her of stage fright, and I'm talking vomiting, laryngitis, the works."

Dr. McCurl smiled, showing off a straight row of super-tiny top teeth.

"Now you make sure she doesn't overdo it," Aunt Ruby said, nudging me toward my mother's chair. I almost tripped over the accordion.

As they were leaving, Dr. McCurl surprised me by reaching out and shaking my hand. His hand was about the same size as mine, which made me feel more grown-up than I wanted to be. I waved him and Aunt Ruby down the driveway and out of sight.

"Close the drapes," Mom said weakly.

"Why?"

"Close them," she said, and turned away, avoiding the light.

I figured she'd earned herself a little darkness. I took one last look along the street. There was hardly anything out there, just Barfy tied up and dozing on the Burrs' front lawn and Lonny Milford picking up grocery store fliers and torn Popsicle wrappers from his front yard.

"Hurry up," she said, her voice flat as a hammered nail.

*

At six o'clock on Saturday, my father, Lissy and I were the first three human beings awake in the whole of Scarborough. The streetlights had dimmed and the dew was so thick the car was covered in hundreds of dime-sized puddles.

We were leaving my Mom behind, still asleep. Everyone's drapes were closed, so our house didn't look any different from the Burrs' or the Remingtons' or the Milfords'. So what if we were only driving to Grey Bay for the day? I was beginning to share my father's need for getaways.

We were supposed to be clearing the bush, hauling out rocks and chopping down trees, but we spent most of our time exploring, imagining our future.

"Here's where the rocking chair will go," Dad said, plopping down into a pile of evergreen branches.

"And here's where I'll sleep," I said, laying myself flat out on a giant moss-covered rock.

Lissy joined in, hugging a small oak tree and singing, "Me, me, me!"

Before we left, I planted my feet firmly apart and took a last long look at the sky. What was there to be afraid of? Falling clouds would be soft and vaporous. They wouldn't hurt at all.

*

In honour of Lissy's seventeenth birthday, my father sprung me from school at noon. First stop, the L & M Restaurant on Danforth, famous for hamburgers that dripped pickles, onions, tomatoes, relish, ketchup and mustard. Then on to Dairy Queen for butterscotch sundaes buried under heaps of nuts.

We picked up Grammie from her one-bedroom apartment on

Woodbine. This was the first time I'd seen her since she walked out on Mom. It surprised me that Dad didn't seem the least bit angry with her, in fact he was acting as if he truly liked her.

Our final destination was Lissy's idea of paradise: the Riverdale Zoo. Zoom, she spotted a peacock and raced off. Zoom, a mountain goat, a camel, a mynah bird, a white wolf, a sloth, a hippopotamus. Lissy couldn't stay in one place for more than thirty seconds. We struggled to keep up with her, to make sure she didn't squeeze between the bars of the anteater's cage.

It took me a while to notice the people around us, how they were watching Lissy the way we were watching the animals, fascinated by the drooling and her cross-eyed look as she tried to see everything at once. The way her arms hung rubbery at her sides. The strange sort of hop and jump she made instead of a normal walk. The wheezy, giggly sound of her voice that turned what she said into gibberish. They were looking at us as well. It was like being frisked by a dozen cops at the same time. Somewhere in the crowd I heard the word "retarded."

"Now I know why Mom's afraid to go outside," I said. We hadn't done ordinary family things in ages.

"What are you talking about?" my father asked.

"She doesn't want people to know she's the mother of a retard."

"What an ugly thing to say," Grammie said, almost spitting. "Lissy has nothing to do with your mother's selfishness."

"She's not selfish," Dad interrupted. "She's ill."

Grammie looked like she was going to laugh, but managed to control herself.

"Ill? Is it a virus, a tumour? Bad behaviour isn't a disease."

By this time we were in the monkey house amidst deafening chatter that made us all raise our voices.

"Don't you understand, people are staring at us," I tried to explain. "Doesn't anyone ever think about me?"

"Like mother, like son," Grammie snorted. "Selfish with a capital S."

"Jesus, don't you have a tender bone anywhere in your body?"

Dad shouted.

"I feel a great tenderness toward Lissy," she shouted back. "She's an angel."

"Stop it," I yelled, louder than the loudest monkey.

We were putting on quite a show. People were staring more openly now and I could feel my cheeks burning. But of course Lissy, the angel, the only one of us who couldn't care less what anyone thought, had already grown tired of the monkey house and was headed for the door.

★

I asked Wendy to take a walk with me after school the next day, across Danforth to the Eli Lily Company's huge front lawn, an ocean of dandelions and clover in May. We shucked off our shoes and squeezed the grass between our toes. We soon wore out such topics as Miss Luther's private life (we decided she was having a long-distance affair with a bomber pilot flying secret missions over Vietnam) and our favourite colours (we both loved blue) and vegetables (hers were peas; mine, creamed corn).

"Tell me more," she said, staring like she was trying to memorize me.

"Like what?" I asked, digging my toes deep into the grass.

"Well…" she said, then paused, as if sorting through a filing cabinet of questions, "what about your father? How's his heart?"

"Fine. Completely fine."

"And your mother?"

"My mother?"

"What does she do?"

I felt ripples in the pit of my belly. I wasn't sure what kind of rumours Wendy might have heard.

"She's a psychologist. She's working on an important theory at the moment."

Barely a dozen words and I had already travelled to a place of no return.

"That's why our front curtains are closed. So she can concentrate."

The only way I was able to stop myself was to bite down on my tongue.

"Wow," Wendy sighed, lapping it up. "My Mom has a part-time job at the Valhalla Theatre, in the ticket booth."

"That sounds like a neat job. I guess she gets to see movies for free." I tried to sound fascinated. Maybe I was fascinated. But my fake mother clearly trumped her real mother.

"And what about your sister?"

Wendy had the open face of someone genuinely interested.

"She's an angel," I said, trying to sound matter-of-fact. I sounded as loony as Mom. But Wendy didn't so much as blink. An angel seemed perfectly credible.

"Is that why she doesn't go to regular school?"

"She doesn't need to. She's a kind of genius."

I couldn't bear to speak and listen to myself at the same time. I was disappearing behind a smokescreen so thick that soon Wendy wouldn't be able to find me.

"What a fascinating life you have."

"C'mon," I said, trying to sound daring, squeezing back into my shoes. "Let's *do* something really fascinating."

I grabbed her hand and we dashed across Danforth to the giant Chevrolet billboard. Marco and I used to scale it back in grade six, yelling "King of the Castle" at the top of our lungs.

"Follow me, you'll love it."

I started climbing the wooden scaffold that led to the narrow ledge. I thought that once I stood next to the glossy picture of that blue Chevy and looked out over the city, the wind would erase all my lies. Maybe Wendy wouldn't follow me out of nerves or dizziness? But she surprised me, tackling the climb as if she were one of the Flying Wallendas, never once looking down.

"Holy cow," she said when she reached the top. "I can see for miles."

"Can you see your own house?" I asked, shielding my eyes

from the sun.

"I can't tell. Every house looks the same."

It felt good to know that from the ledge of the billboard, 6 Arizona Avenue was one of hundreds of tiny Scarborough bungalows. Nothing about it stood out. It was as normal as any other house.

"Every house is my house," Wendy giggled.

"Every house is mine as well," I said. We were like a King and Queen looking down on our own kingdom.

I pictured Mom sitting quietly inside one of those dream houses like one of Lissy's Barbie dolls.

*

On the day of our next expedition to Grey Bay, I slept in a little and had to rush through a bowl of Shreddies. Mom stood by the stove, drinking coffee. What was she doing up so early?

"What's going on?"

Dad was sitting at his usual spot at the kitchen table, chugging orange juice.

"Guess who's coming with us?" He grinned like an idiot, with bits of orange pulp stuck to his moustache. "None other than the beautiful Flo Tedley!" He sounded bogus and loud like a TV announcer. This would probably turn out to be nothing but a trick.

But one look at the car was enough to convince me. Dad had turned the Valiant into a hearse. A couple of dark blue beach towels were duct taped over the back window, the two side windows were covered by several layers of newspaper. Between the front and back seats he had hung a curtain rod, and a pair of heavy black drapes divided the interior in two. The side mirror was the only way he had to check traffic from the rear.

The car was pulled almost into the yard so none of the neighbours could see. Dad carried Mom out, a green flannel sheet covering everything but her ankles and feet. He told Lissy and me to scramble into the front. I didn't dare peek through the curtains to see what Mom was doing. It was so quiet back there, I wondered whether she'd already died of fright. I had the creepiest feeling that we were going to bury her somewhere on the Grey Bay property.

Once we were out of Toronto, Dad began to sing his favourite old songs, and Lissy tunelessly joined in. "Once in Love with Amy," "All of Me," "The Red River Valley." He jabbed me playfully in the ribs. We were on the outskirts of Peterborough when we heard Mom joining in. *By the light of the silvery moon,* she sang, her small voice muffled by the curtains. Dad added harmony while Lissy wailed around the edges. They sang several songs this way, ending up with "Mares eat oats and does eat oats and little lambs eat ivy," though they forgot most of the words and had to join Lissy in her stream of nonsense. Even while Dad parked the car at the edge of our Grey Bay lot, we stayed put until they finished "Shine On Harvest Moon." Three chipmunks were playing a frantic game of tag up a tree.

"All right, already," Dad laughed, flinging his door open. "Come on."

I knew she'd never get out. Still, I gave her the entire morning and afternoon. No matter whether I was raking or hefting or chopping or fighting off the first of the season's blackflies, I kept one eye on the car, as did Dad. We didn't have as much fun as on other trips. We didn't shout or laugh, we were careful not to push the day into something wild. Every once in a while Dad checked in with Mom, passing her some things, removing others. I saw him empty a jar full of pee.

We left for home around four in the afternoon. Lissy dropped off to sleep before we reached Havelock, missing several fields of cows and one groundhog sitting on the shoulder of the road. Dad tried to start another sing-along, but his voice soon trailed off.

*

Lissy and I were in the thick of a cereal fight the next morning when Mom sauntered into the kitchen. Lissy's forehead was plastered with wet Shreddies and my pajama top was blotchy with milk stains. Dad had a Shreddie on his chest, though he was trying to ignore us behind the June *Popular Mechanics*.

"Morning all," Mom said, not bothering to scold us for messing up her kitchen. She was wearing her pink kimono over a darker pink nightgown and her hair was in curlers, her usual Sunday morning getup. She was also wearing a pair of beige sunglasses.

My father cocked his head like a confused dog.

"Morning, babe," he said. He didn't so much as glance at her again. Lissy giggled.

I tried to think of something I could say that would make Mom feel singled out, but I didn't have the voice for it, didn't have the control. *Why the fucking glasses?* was what I was thinking. But that would only have got me a rolled up *Popular Mechanics* across the head.

I ended up not saying anything. After all, wasn't she supposed to be in disguise? I walked out, careful not to brush against her.

SIX

LISSY AND I WERE INVITED to Grammie's for dinner. She had something important she wanted to say to us. I'd been wishing she'd return to Arizona Avenue, even though what she wanted to say probably had something to do with my bad posture or Lissy's specialness. I worried about the public bus ride. Lissy was bound to draw a lot of attention and make me feel like a freak.

The bus was less than half full. We sat in the back and I kept one hand on Lissy's knee, giving her a little pinch every time she squirmed. Only once did she speak out loud, when she noticed the photo of a whale on one of the ads, but the other passengers ignored her.

The food at Grammie's was better than I'd expected, her spaghetti with meat sauce not half bad, and the rice pudding smothered in cinnamon was great. I even managed to keep my spine straight and my elbows off the edge of the table, which meant that Grammie left me alone and showered all her attention on Lissy. I stayed perfect through the drying of the dishes, perfect right into Grammie's living room, where I perched on the edge of her lumpy armchair, my hands folded in my lap. An hour to go before Dad arrived to take us home. If I were super nice, maybe she'd let me watch TV.

"Your china figurines look beautiful," I said. Grammie usually loved to tell stories about where she'd found the old street peddler with his yellow and green balloons, or the ballerina with a single red rose in her hair. But tonight she didn't respond to the compliments.

"The apartment's getting crowded," she complained. "I feel like a canary in a cage."

Excited by the word canary, Lissy rushed to the apartment door.

"Out," she said.

"Hush," Grammie snapped. "Now listen here. I want you to know something important. Your mother and father are not good parents at the moment. If there's one thing you can count on, it's that things always get worse before they get better."

"Okay," I said.

Had Mom called and complained about me? Had Dad blamed me for adding to the weight of his burdens?

"There's nothing you can do about them, do you understand? They will continue to please themselves no matter what you or Lissy need."

"Okay," I repeated. I had to clench my jaws in order not to say something rude. No matter how angry I was at my parents, Grammie's attacks made me want to stand up for them.

She gave me a bit of a fish eye, then continued.

"All you need to concern yourself with is your sister. Make sure she's clean and fed, no matter what else is going on around you. You've got to take care of this treasure. She's your responsibility now."

"Okay," I said for the third time.

"I'm taking a vacation," she said. "Doris Nealon, Ethel McAllister and me. July and August."

At first I thought she meant she was taking a break from checking in with Dad or Aunt Ruby.

"I'm going to Europe. A jet plane to London," she said, "the Netherlands, Belgium, Germany, Austria, Hungary, Yugoslavia,

Greece, Italy, Switzerland, France, then back to England again." She counted off each destination on her fingers, using up all ten then starting again.

I tried to imagine Grammie asking for a cup of tea in a dozen different languages.

"How will you get around?"

"A tour bus," she said. "I hear it's as comfortable as a rocking chair."

Grammie would be the first of our family to cross an ocean. Both Dad and Uncle Maurice had sat out World War Two—Dad's hernia and my Uncle Maurice's slipped disc. Uncle Frank had joined the army, but only made it as far as Winnipeg.

My mother was wearing sunglasses in the house, and Grammie would soon be weaving her way across a new continent.

"So I have to look after Lissy?" I asked, trying to sum up the entire conversation.

She forced me to swear on her hardcover copy of *The Agony and the Ecstasy* that I would do what I was told.

"If anything bad happens to our girl, you'll have me to answer to."

*

Middle of the night, Grey Bay, our first sleepover, Dad and I side by side in a brand new camouflage pup tent. Our small campfire was smouldering. Judging by the hoarseness of Dad's breathing, he was asleep. I wasn't so lucky. Animal noises were keeping me awake.

The hoot of an owl reminded me of someone at a seance reciting a dead person's name over and over. Twigs snapped, then there was a sort of gush, like breath blown into a giant wooden flute. A faint whistle. Water dripping, or was it blood? Fear grabbed hold of my legs in the sleeping bag and twisted them into painful knots. Everything was exactly the way horror comics describe it: heart thumping, hands shaking. Major doom. Numbness spread through me. My balls shrank. What if I were eaten alive by a bear? What if the angry ghost of a long-dead Indian brave scalped me with an invisible tomahawk? Was this what had happened to Mom, one fear multiplying into many? Or was it her fault that I was thinking these deadly thoughts? Had her terrors leaked out and infected the whole of Grey Bay?

A long, tortured cry sounded over the water. I opened my mouth and gurgled when I meant to yelp. I rolled my sleeping bag across the narrow tent, smack into Dad. He stirred a little, mumbling, and then pushed back against me, his legs touching mine, his breath in my face. I laid there, holding my own breath, concentrating on the soft sounds coming from Dad rather than the racket outside. Slowly I began to breathe again, taking on his courage. When the cry rang out a second time, I realized I was an asshole. Stupid, stupid fear. Only a loon. I closed my eyes and imagined that each of my father's breaths was blowing us across Grey Bay, across the entire country, that come morning we'd find ourselves at least halfway to somewhere very far away.

*

Marco dropped by the night after I got home from the sleepover, and we sat on the front porch, watching Dad clip the hedge, creating a perfectly flat ledge of green.

"Gee whiz, your Dad can sure cut a straight line." Marco whistled, hypnotized by the flashing of the shears.

Good eyes, good arms. All traces of heart attack vanished. He looked young and powerful, like an older brother.

"You should see him up at Grey Bay," I said. "He practically tears out whole trees with his bare hands."

Mr. Morelli was a short, stubby man with eyebrows so thick they hung down over his eyes like bangs. Marco would probably come to resemble him in alarming ways. His English wasn't that great. His communications mostly sounded like grunts to me. Marco wasn't exactly ashamed of him, but saved his praise for his mother, who, he said, could carry a stack of laundry as tall as she was or cook spaghetti for a hundred relatives at a time.

"Imagine if my mother and your father got together," Marco said. "Like Wonder Woman and Superman."

I liked to lose myself in Marco's imagination when he wasn't being totally gross. I pictured Dad carving the shape of a lightning bolt into the hedge, Mrs. Morelli at his side in a fireproof apron.

"Hey, look." Marco said, jabbing me in the ribs. "Lonny's Dad."

Mr. Milford was shambling across the street, bent over like the Hunchback of Notre Dame.

"You trying to show up the neighbourhood?" he called out to my father.

"How's it going, Dave?" Dad boomed like the Friendly Giant, laying his shears down on top of the hedge.

"Fine, Ed, just fine."

"Get a load of his skin," Marco whispered. "He looks blue."

"Those are his veins showing through," I explained. "He's got cancer."

"It better not be catching," Marco said after a long, serious pause. "Your Dad's standing pretty close."

But both of us were sure we didn't have to worry about my father. He was one hundred percent alive. He placed one of his hands on Mr. Milford's shoulder, a keep-hanging-in-there kind of clasp. I wondered if Marco could feel the energy flowing through his body the same way I could feel it in mine.

★

The first June hot spell arrived, and by seven o'clock in the evening every porch on Arizona Avenue was a front row seat. Since Dad was still at the Texaco, Lissy and I shared our own top step. We had a perfect view of everyone across the street, starting with Mr. Milford and Lonny, who sat on kitchen chairs, staring off into space, ignoring each other, as if they were miles apart. Next door,

86

Franny and Lucy Remington were sharing a textbook, cramming for their grade nine exams, while their mother, making a rare public appearance, sat behind them reading one of her Jehovah's Witness magazines. The entire Burr family overflowed from their porch. Mrs. Burr and Linda were fanning themselves with homemade paper fans. At the Costellos', Diana was paging steadily through her Harlequin.

Everything was quiet, until Mr. Costello's slurred voice came echoing down his driveway.

"Bloody lazy, the lot of you, letting your bloody yards go to ruin."

The only ruined yard on the street was the Costellos'. We could hear his push mower, clattering toward the street. When he staggered into view he was totally naked.

There was a sort of communal whoosh as we all gasped. Mr. Costello reached the edge of his property, dick and balls bouncing. He swung his ass around, shoving the mower in a crooked row all the way across his lawn. If Dad had been there, he would have rushed across the street and wrapped his shirt around Mr. Costello's blubbery waist.

Diana screamed, "I can't take this anymore!" and started hitting herself on the head with her paperback. Everyone sat paralyzed, watching her beat herself up for a good twenty seconds until finally Mrs. Burr had had enough.

"For God's sake, someone do something," she cried.

Lonny Milford was the first to act, sprinting across the Remingtons' lawn. He and Mr. Burr arrived at the Costellos' at the same time. Mr. Costello dropped the mower handle and flailed his arms about. He was crazy drunk. Mr. Burr manhandled him in his tough cop way, trying not to get too close, while Lonny didn't even seem aware that Mr. Costello was naked, putting an arm around his shoulder and slowly leading him away.

Diana disappeared into the house. How much courage must it take to fall apart in front of everyone? I wondered what it would feel like to flop down on the sidewalk and let loose, kicking my heels against the curb and refusing to stop.

Once Lonny had made sure that Mr. Costello was safely inside, he came across the street to join Lissy and me. I wondered if he expected me to say something darkly meaningful, as Dad might have done had he been there to witness it all.

"What a life," was all I could manage.

"Beg your pardon?" Lonny said quietly out of the corner of his mouth.

I tried to be clearer. "Mr. Costello. Being an alcoholic is sad." I really wanted to say something about how struck I was by his tenderness toward Mr. Costello, but couldn't figure out how to do that without sounding like a suck-up.

"He doesn't need your pity."

"I wasn't pitying him," I said. It felt like danger was in the air, but I couldn't stop myself. What if my mother had done something that blatant? How would she be able to show her face outside again?

"It sure sounded like pity to me." Lonny looked at me as if the word were written across my forehead. "What do you know about anyone's life other than your own?"

"I don't have to understand something to have a feeling about it."

"What a fucking lamebrain thing to say." He was standing so close to me that I could feel his spittle on my face.

"Why are you being so mean?" I asked, afraid that sounded like a six-year-old. "I meant to say that sometimes life can be tough."

"You talk like you're above it all. Poor Mr. Costello, you groan. Makes your heart bleed, does it?" He was leaning even closer in. Another half an inch and he could bite my nose. "I could pull your pants down right here and now," he sneered. "Underneath it all, you're as pathetic as Mr. Costello."

"You're the one who's pathetic," I spat, trying to deflect attention from the pathetic in my life.

"You little prick." Lonny's face had gone red.

Lissy must have been feeling wildly uncomfortable with all the tension in the air. She let out a giggle that hardly sounded retarded at all. She was dressed younger than most seventeen-year-olds, in pink terrycloth shorts and a white blouse printed with red suckers, but her body wasn't that different from Franny's and Lucy's. I saw Lonny glance at her unbuttoned top button.

I put my arm around Lissy, pulling her hard against me. "Stop staring at my sister's breasts," I said.

"You think I've got the hots for a retard?"

"What do I know? I'm a lamebrain."

Although Lonny was doing the fuming, it was me who felt like I was about to go up in smoke.

He gave me a steely look, then turned to Lissy and said in a sweet voice, "Your brother's a dead man, sugar," before walking away.

★

That evening Dad sent me out to pick up a quart of milk, though what I was really doing was taking Lissy for a walk. We took a shortcut through the schoolyard, playing Follow the Leader. I marched like a soldier, whistling Beatles' songs, swinging my head back and forth to each beat. Lissy was a great copycat, but she had some trouble with whistling because her mouth refused to shape itself into an O. It sounded like she was blowing raspberries. For the walk home, I bought her a grape Mr. Freezie.

She sucked noisily, the purple staining her mouth. Suddenly, she lowered the Mr. Freezie and giggled low in her throat. Lonny Milford was waiting for us by the schoolyard gate, slouched against the chain-link fence, loose and dangerous.

"Well, well, if it isn't Lissy's sissy," he called out when I was still a good six feet away. "Who are you pitying today?"

"Out of our way," I said, trying to sound like the monosyllabic good guy in *Shane*.

"Big mouth," Lonny said, gritting his teeth. For a second, I thought he was going to hiss. "Too bad you're still such a runt."

He charged me, head down, like a bull. In an instant, I was on the ground. He dropped to his knees and straddled me, grinding down on my cheek with his knuckles, his hot, smoky breath on my face.

He climbed off me and straightened his shirt. One of his knuckles was bloody. "Now it's just me and your sister. What do you think, sweetheart? Does he pity you sometimes too?"

It was clear that Lissy wasn't sure what to think. Marco and I often roughhoused when she was around. She was staring down at me as if my face contained the alphabet that would explain what was happening.

I lifted myself up on one elbow and kicked out, first my right leg, then my left, missing Lonny by at least six inches.

"You're still a pervert," I said, tasting blood on the tip of my tongue.

Pulling myself up to a full sitting position, I snatched a fistful of dirt and threw it at him, which caused him to kick his own cloud of dirt and pebbles back at me.

"Everyone pities you," I said, loud and clear.

He landed a kick on my thigh as I was struggling to get back on my feet. One last boot split the milk carton, a shockingly white stream flowing onto the dirt. Then he turned back to Lissy, who was torn between Lonny's attentions and the puddle of milk slowly turning brown.

"You want to come home with me, honey?" he asked, reaching out and taking her by the wrist.

I screamed at the top of my lungs, forcing myself between them. "Pervert!" Then I screamed again.

He lunged at me. "Shut the fuck up," he said.

"Pervert," I repeated even louder, my throat burning. I wasn't thinking about what he might do to Lissy, but about Mom's panic and Dad's anger. How would I ever explain letting Lonny steal her?

By this time, about half a dozen parents from the houses across from the schoolyard were coming to investigate. I didn't know any of them by name, but they'd probably seen Lissy and me walking home from Kingston Road many times. Lonny was the obvious bad guy here.

"What the hell's going on?" someone asked.

"Why don't you find someone your own size," another said, faking a punch at Lonny's belly.

"Okay, okay," Lonny said. He turned to me and added, "No hard feelings, kid," an apology of sorts, which seemed to satisfy everyone. He kept his head down as he walked through the small circle of neighbours and out toward the gate.

I couldn't tell my parents what really happened. Mom would have had a fit and Dad would have reacted to the fit by blaming me for being in the wrong place at the wrong time. So I told them I was climbing the monkey bars in the schoolyard, showing off for Lissy, and slipped. I'd crushed the milk carton when I landed. But when Marco heard that Lonny Milford had given me a fat lip, he was hot for revenge.

"We'll be like the Mafia," he said.

Sure, revenge felt like a good idea, but nothing I could dream up seemed credible. My first choice would have been to cut off Lonny's hand at the wrist with one whack of an axe. I could see all that spouting blood. Or maybe blind him, poke a lit cigarette right into an open eye.

"It's useless, Marco," I said, imagining myself in a cell while a disfigured Lonny Milford continued to say twisted things to Lissy.

But Marco had the mind and the stubbornness of an eight-year-old.

"I've got it," he said. "The perfect punishment for an asshole." We met after dark in the shadowy part of the Burrs' driveway. Marco had brought along a plastic beach pail and shovel, as well as a half-empty roll of paper towel. I came equipped with one of Dad's flashlights and a pair of Mom's pink rubber gloves. Louie Burr was empty-handed, so we put him in charge of following Barfy. Our plan was to start with Dakota Drive, then head north up Virginia Street and left on Maine Road, until we were back on

Arizona. If anyone spotted us, we'd say we were cleaning up the streets.

In 1966, for the most part, dogs were allowed to roam free. For the next hour, we collected poodle shit and collie shit and even some poorly buried cat shit. Dachshund shit, terrier shit and good old-fashioned mutt shit. Louie found what he swore was squirrel shit, but it looked like rabbit pellets to me. By the time we got back to the Burrs' driveway, the pail was almost full. We topped it up with the shit of Barfy's free-range area, although some of the older shit was too hard to use. Barfy was helpful, dumping a brand new steaming pile practically at Louie's feet. Marco was so excited by our haul that he suggested adding a few turds of his own, but Louie and I nixed that.

"Let's get it over with," I said, worried that since it was after nine, our parents' last-week-of-school permissiveness might be wearing thin.

We left Barfy in the backyard, behind the closed gate. Starting with the Milfords' front stoop, we plastered a pathway of shit all the way to Lonny's souped-up white Chevy. At first we were a bit squeamish about getting any of the shit on ourselves, but before long we were plopping shit on the hood, even smearing some on the windshield. Marco noticed that the driver's door was unlocked, and bingo! we swung it open and dumped fresh Barfy shit all over the seat. We ditched the rubber gloves, pushing them through the sewer grate in front of the Milfords' and washed the pail and shovel under the Burrs' hose.

Later, lying in bed, my heart wouldn't stop pounding. What a release it was to feel those bongo drums deep inside my body! Did I sleep? I must have. I was at the living room window by six the next morning, spreading the curtains far enough to peer past the crabapple tree, watching the sun as it rose on Lonny Milford's trail of shit. It didn't look that impressive from a distance, but I knew it would be disgusting enough to send Lonny into a full-fledged fit. At seven, the Milfords' front door finally opened and Lonny stepped out, right into the first pile. He hopped around the porch on one foot, trying to kick the shit off the other. He looked like he was swearing. He leaned against the iron railing, still kicking, and followed the trail of shit with his eyes all the way to the Chevy. His mouth fell open like a breadbox door. He leapt off the porch and dashed to the car. He threw his head back a couple of times, slammed his hands down hard on the hood and kicked his own front tire.

I could have stayed safe at the window, but I wanted to get as close to his anger as possible, to feel it soaking into me. Keeping my eyes on the Chevy's fins, I crossed the street. By the time I reached his sidewalk I'd worked myself up to a stride. Lonny was so busy swearing and stomping, he might not have noticed me had I simply breezed by.

"Jesus Christ," I said, startling him. "Is that shit?"

He glared at me. "What do you know about this, you little puke."

"I don't have a clue."

Be brave, be bold, I told myself.

"You had something to do with this, I know it, you little motherfucker. I'll fucking break your neck."

"You don't know me that well," I said. "I wouldn't go near shit with a ten-foot pole."

A guy like Lonny must have tons of enemies. Once he'd thought it over, I figured he'd come up with lots of possible culprits. Besides, he probably wouldn't think I'd be dumb enough to show my face. What kind of crazy fool would return to the scene of the crime just to gloat?

He eyeballed me thoroughly as if a shit-smearing double agent was lurking beneath my innocent mask. I managed to control every nerve, kept my jaw squared. I didn't so much as twitch an eyelash. Not showing fear was almost as good as not feeling it.

But when I went back home and resumed my position at the front window, watching Lonny scrape and hose away the shit, his aloneness made me feel guilty and sad. What a creepy thing Marco, Louie and I had done. How far would I go to escape from fear, to make sure someone else got saddled with all the humiliation?

"What's so interesting out there?" Dad asked, just out of bed and heading toward the kitchen.

"Nothing," I lied. "Just a couple of squirrels playing tag in the crabapple." I wanted to keep my feelings about Lonny to myself.

*

After saying goodbye to Miss Luther, showering her with a bunch of cheap gifts—Evening In Paris talcum powder, Black Magic chocolates, nylon scarves—the grade eight graduating class marched out of Kingston Road Public School, an army of thirteen- and fourteen-year-olds heading for what grown-ups loved to call the future. I felt as if I were abandoning little pieces of myself and would never be completely put back together again.

Wendy was waiting for me, liar and shit disturber that I was.

"I'm leaving tomorrow on holidays," she said. She looked like she might start crying. "My parents are making me go to the Maritimes. Can we take a walk?"

We walked south of Kingston Road to Valhalla Park and its great view of Lake Ontario. I liked who I was when I was with Wendy, lies aside. She made me feel like I made a difference in her life. Standing there on the edge of the Bluffs, the water down below us chemistry-set green, the clouds above us green around the edges, all I could think to do was tell her the truth.

"I'm really sorry you have to go away," I began.

"I'm glad you're sorry."

Scarborough Bluffs was the right place for the truth. If I saw disgust in Wendy's eyes, I could step off the edge of the cliff and plummet to the beach below.

"I need to tell you some stuff," I said, kicking at the uneven ground. "I was afraid you wouldn't like me if you knew that my sister Lissy is mentally retarded. If I told you my mother isn't a psychologist. Actually, she's nowhere near normal. Our drapes are closed all the time because she's afraid of things. A doctor comes

94

to see her every week, but she refuses to go outside."

My hands were shaking hard. I tried to slip them behind my back, but Wendy grabbed one and curled it in one of her own. She had a worried look on her face.

"And your father?" she finally asked.

Dad was a breeze. "He's one hundred percent true. Heart attack, Texaco, the works. I didn't have to make him up."

She nodded slowly. "Lissy probably is an angel in some ways," she said. "And your mother might still become a psychologist once she gets over her fears."

She looked beautiful standing there at the edge of the Bluffs like Nancy Drew after solving a mystery. I didn't know what else to say. The rest of the truth lay off in the distance. I didn't have a clue how to get there other than to let Wendy go off to the Maritimes and wait for her to come home. I took a deep breath, then leaned forward and placed my sore lip on Wendy Fergie's soft lips, a new, improved way of talking.

★

No matter how much chopping and digging and clearing we did, Grey Bay remained a wilderness. But I wasn't afraid of furry black spiders anymore, or of the bumblebees that zoomed past my face, or crayfish in the shallows, or loon cries, or rustling leaves. Mid-afternoon, after hours of slugging it out with various tree stumps, Dad asked if I wanted to go skinny-dipping. At first I thought about water snakes and muskies. But before I had time to dream up all sorts of horror stories, a voice rose in my mind: *are you going to let snakes run your life?*

I tossed my shirt onto the beach and pulled off my pants and underwear in one big sweep. I took a running leap and did a cannonball into the Bay. The water was so cold, I almost panicked, but then I saw Dad sailing over my head in a glorious, naked dive.

"Aargghh," he screamed when his head broke the surface of the water. I laughed and laughed.

SEVEN

LISSY AND I WERE LYING on the living room rug with the comics section of the *Toronto Star* spread out in front of us.

"Gammie!" Lissy exclaimed, as Grammie came walking through the front door, shedding a cape of sunlight behind her.

"It's awfully dark in here," she said, entering the living room and banging a knee into Mom's orange chair.

I helped her to sit then brought her a glass of lemonade. Mom joined us, still wearing her sunglasses. She stared at Grammie as if seeing a mirage.

"I hope you don't mind my dropping by like this, but as I guess you know I'm off to Europe on Monday. I thought we should make our peace."

Mom didn't seem to be listening. She couldn't take her eyes off a trickle of sunlight making its way through a crack in the drapes and causing the bottom of Grammie's glass to shimmer.

"There are a few little details I'd like to get straight. If I should get sick in one of those foreign countries, I don't want to have to fly home all alone. I've already talked to Veronica and Ruby about flying over, but if both of them were indisposed, I was thinking maybe you could spare Ed. If the plane crashes, then I'd like a small tombstone erected in St. John's Cemetery with *Eternal Joy* on it, something like that. Ed can take care of it."

The skin above and below Mom's sunglasses turned paler than usual.

"Let me see now," Grammie continued. "My will is in the safety deposit box at my bank. Most of my jewellery is to go to Veronica and Ruby. You wouldn't have anywhere to wear it."

It was clear to me that Grammie was trying to hurt Mom. A part of me cheered her meanness on. Maybe she'd succeed in dragging my mother outside where Dad and Aunt Ruby had failed. But I also felt sorry for Mom. Grammie didn't fight fair.

"I hope you have a good time," Mom said, finally. She was slouching in her chair as if one more dig would send her sprawling onto the rug. "And that you come home safe and sound."

"No thanks to you." Grammie harrumphed.

"Me?"

"If you had your way, you'd have me falling out of the sky before I even get to Europe."

Mom opened her mouth to disagree, but she lacked the logic and strength to go head to head with Grammie.

"Well, I'm off," Grammie announced, rising from her chair. She threw her arms around Lissy, squeezed a quack out of her then slapped me on the back a couple of times. Mom tried to get between Grammie and the front door, her arms stretched out for a hug of her own, but Grammie slid past, leaving her with nothing in her arms but air.

★

It was the hottest night of the year. Even the walls were sweating. It was the kind of heat that made me feel the weight of each hair on my head. When Dad first appeared at the foot of my bed, I thought he was a mirage.

"Go away," I mumbled, my tongue thick and dry.

"Robby, Robby," he persisted. He was wearing only his underpants. His chest was sweaty. "I need your help."

He led me to my parent's bedroom, where a fan was aimed at the pillows. Mom was huddled against the headboard, wrapped up to her neck in a soggy sheet. I wondered for a moment whether she was having a heart attack.

"Tell her that Grammie's plane flew away safely," Dad pleaded.

She started to cry, each sob more hoarse than the one before.

"She's dead, isn't she? The plane crashed, I know it."

"She's had a bad dream," my father explained. "Tell her what's real, Robby."

Real? All I could think was that it was ninety degrees in the house, that my mother was crazy and my father helpless, that it was the middle of the night. Europe and death were two entirely different places.

I spoke like a robot. "I saw Grammie's plane take off."

"She's been in Europe for over twelve hours now. A postcard is on its way."

"But I saw her falling from the sky. She was on fire."

"You didn't actually see that," Dad said, in a singsong voice that made my skin crawl. "You dreamt it."

"A nightmare," I added.

"The heat does all sorts of weird things," Dad continued, hitching his underpants high. "Right now I feel like there's a camel snorting down the back of my neck."

Eventually Mom stopped crying but she still looked scared.

"Where is she in Europe?" she asked in a little girl voice.

"Can I go back to bed now?" I interrupted.

"You better be right," she said. It sounded like a threat.

A flash of anger blazed in my chest. "I wish her fucking plane had crashed into our house," I said in the robot voice.

Dad pushed me hard and sent me stumbling from the room. "Goddamn you, Robby. What an evil thing to say."

★

Hot or not, Dr. McCurl wore a suit jacket and a tie whenever he came to see Mom. Last time he'd worn big black oxfords that reminded me of snow tires. Despite the fact that they'd been meeting once a week, everything remained strangely formal between them. Dr. McCurl always sat on the edge of his chair.

I'd heard things about Mom's childhood before, but it was fascinating to hear Dr. McCurl make connections between her memories and her agoraphobia. For example, with two older sisters used to fighting for their share of attention, Mom often chose to keep quiet. She learned to wait things out, keep her feelings to herself.

"I think we're ready for a little progress," Dr. McCurl said. "Step by step," he continued. "We're going to try a little something called systematic desensitization, a fancy name for some simple behavioural therapy."

Mom had made herself small in a corner of the couch. In her blue and white striped sundress, with her blonde hair tied into a knot on the top of her head and the big sunglasses pressed tight against her eyes, she looked like a giant three-year-old, like Lissy's twin sister.

"I think I've already faced enough fear for today," she said.

"Talking about your past isn't one of your fears."

"Well, it must be the heat then. I really am done in." She lifted a limp wrist and wiped sweat from her forehead with the back of her hand.

Dr. McCurl stood up, spine straight, shoulders rolled back. He snatched off the sunglasses.

"Natural light is good for the system," he declared, reminding me of the educational films Miss Luther used to show us in Botany and Biology. Pocketing the sunglasses, Dr. McCurl walked over to the living room window, placing one hand on each drape.

"Don't," she said. "Why can't you understand? I don't want my furniture bleached by the sun."

Dr. McCurl pulled each drape and sheer open about an inch. A bright stripe of sunlight shot across the rug.

"There," he said. "A small step."

Mom had shut her eyes, but I saw her take a peek. Shut, open, shut, open, this went on for several seconds until the telephone rang.

"Oh my God," she cried. "They're calling to tell me my mother is dead." She covered her eyes with her hands as if Grammie were lying dead before her.

Dr. McCurl wasn't fazed. He ordered me to answer the phone, and demanded that Mom get a grip. He wouldn't allow so much as a snivel. When I returned, Mom was sitting quietly again, her eyes wide, light pooling around her feet.

"It was Aunt Ruby," I said. "Just checking in."

"An ordinary phone call," Dr. McCurl said, nodding his head.

Mom was blinking normally now. Dr. McCurl told her that she was to leave the drapes and sheers exactly the way they were until their next session. He put her sunglasses on the coffee table, and then shook her hand, sealing the pact.

I glared at her for a moment, then went into the bathroom and ran cold water over my head. When I returned, Dr. McCurl was gone and she had pushed her favourite armchair up against the space between the curtains, which blocked a bit of the light. She was wearing her sunglasses again.

*

Dad's forty-seventh birthday, the temperature ninety-nine degrees in the shade. Lissy and I gave him a Styrofoam ice chest to transport food to and from Grey Bay, as well as a book on how to build your own boat. I'd taken the bus to Shopper's World and had chosen his gifts all on my own. Mom made him an angel food cake with peach icing. The last time Young's Food Market made a delivery, Mr. Young had carried the bags of groceries to our kitchen table and had sorted them into food groups, trying to be of some help.

Mom told Dad she'd been doing some "serious thinking," which she hoped would result in something good for the two of them. We were sitting at the dining room table, the electric fan blowing from its perch on top of the china cabinet. Mom was wearing her sunglasses again, pushed down low on her nose, but her gaze was fully visible, and troubling.

"Serious thinking sounds a lot like worry to me," Dad said, through a mouthful of cake. As far as I knew, he'd never said the word agoraphobia, referring to the fear as her "problem."

Mom was wringing her hands beside her untouched plate of cake.

"No," she said, "not worry. Constructive thinking, Dr. McCurl calls it. If I can understand how this whole thing started, I could change." She didn't seem convinced by her own words, but she kept on, almost whispering. "I could go outside again."

Lissy squirmed a little at the mention of outside, but I stared her down.

"If that's what you want," Dad said. It was clear that he was worrying regardless of what she chose to call it.

"I've been thinking about how I was the baby of the family. Even Ruby and Veronica babied me. They were more like mothers than sisters. I hardly ever had to do anything on my own." She furrowed her brow as if these thoughts were difficult to collect. "I was babied right up until my wedding day."

"I never babied you," my father said.

"Of course you didn't. You've been wonderful. It's just that I went from being babied to being a housewife. Arizona Avenue became my whole world. Days would go by when I wouldn't even look out the window. I was so caught up in trying to make everything right."

"Sounds like women's lib," my father said, paling.

"No," she insisted. "I was the one who chose to stay home." She was straightening her fork and spoon, drawing them together. "Somehow over these last ten years I forgot how to deal with the rest of the world. The six o'clock news started to scare me. People I'd meet on the street on my way to the grocery store seemed to know something I didn't. One day, walking along Kingston Road in broad daylight, I started wondering what would happen if a car began to follow me or a stranger grabbed my arm. I had no idea what I'd do."

"How can anyone know something like that?" Dad said. He kept dabbing at a corner of his mouth where he'd already wiped away a smear of frosting.

"But I'm so out of practice," she explained. "Inside this house, day after day, nothing bad can happen."

Dad began to sound like he always did when he was running out of tolerance and wanted the conversation to stop.

"Living a life full of the unexpected isn't all it's cracked up to be."

"Ed," she said, putting her finger to her lips as if to shush him. "Dr. McCurl and I are really working hard and I'm beginning to understand. This is my birthday gift to you," she concluded. "I'm going to try very hard."

Dad tried to smile but couldn't lose his frown.

"What about here? Will all this go to pot?" He pointed at the cake crumbs, the polished hardwood floor, at Lissy, at me.

Mom reached across the table, the buttons on her blouse brushing her plate. She laid a trembling hand on his cheek.

"Oh, Ed, of course not," she said.

Lissy had had enough. She eked out a bird-like cheep and followed it with a big dog growl. I fought back the urge to do the same, but louder. Mom passed her cake over to Lissy, which immediately calmed her down. I asked to be excused, dashed to the bathroom, turned on the sink taps wide open and cheeped and growled until I too calmed down.

*

Dad and I arrived home from a trip to Canadian Tire the next evening, to find Mom in a panic.

"Lissy's been gone for over an hour," she said, sobbing.

Lissy had been sticking close to home lately, refusing most outings, playing with Queen Mary, sitting on the back porch and waving at the birds in the red maple, close enough to hear Mom calling her through the screen door. She was missing Grammie badly, and her sadness had sunk into depression.

Dad climbed back into the car and headed out to search the streets. I aimed straight for the schoolyard where most of the local action happened after dusk. Sure enough, I spotted her instantly, at the other end of the yard, swinging, surrounded by a bunch of high school kids. I took a deep breath and chanted *bold* under my breath. *Bold, bold, bold.* Crossing the yard, I did my best not to look like one of the walking dead from *Invasion of the Body Snatchers*.

"Lissy," I said sharply, "time to go home."

She was sailing high on the swing, pushed by a short chubby girl whose eyelashes were either fake or caked with mascara. She ignored me completely. Lonny Milford was one of the gang, and he drew nearer to me, sniffing as if I might smell of dog shit.

"She's with us," the girl with the eyelashes said, pushing Lissy even higher.

"If it was up to me, you could have her for keeps," I said, "but my father goes a little crazy when Lissy isn't around."

"She's having fun," Lonny said. "No one is pitying her."

"She'll be home when she's finished her swing," said a thick-necked guy with a sneer like Lonny's. He reminded me of a pit bull.

"Fine with me," I said, starting to back away. Raising my voice a bit, I added, "I guess I'll have to play with the bunnies all by myself."

"Bunnies?" Lonny repeated. "What the hell are you talking about?"

"Bunnies!" Lissy cried, jumping off the swing in mid-air and landing right beside me. She almost knocked me over.

The high schoolers looked confused, but didn't try to stop us from leaving.

When we walked into the house, Mom was sitting on the couch, shaking from head to toe. She could hardly form a sentence. "Where was she?" she finally blurted.

"The schoolyard," I said, making it sound as innocent as a

sandbox. I knew that any details about high school kids would turn her shivers into shudders.

"Bunnies, bunnies," Lissy was chanting.

"Bunnies?" Mom looked as terrified as if I'd said "tarantula" or "snake."

"Bunnies." I tried showing how harmless everything had turned out to be by putting both of my hands above my head and wiggling my fingers. I wiggled and wiggled the bunny ears until finally Lissy squealed with delight.

Mom didn't look convinced.

*

I'd been climbing Scarborough Bluffs for half a day with Marco, Louie and Dana, and arrived home to find Dr. McCurl in high gear.

"Today, Mrs. Tedley, we tackle the back porch."

Mom was refusing to look at him. She had her chin tucked into her collarbone as if playing the accordion. She'd been wearing her sunglasses off and on throughout the week, but they were off now. The glasses had become a kind of thermometer constantly measuring the temperature of her fear.

"Imagine how you'd feel if you found yourself in Africa. Imagine the heat, the circling buzzards. Imagine the roar of a lion, the mad laugh of a hyena."

Mom closed her eyes. "I'd be terrified," she said.

"How terrified?"

"I'd die of fright."

Dr. McCurl seemed overjoyed at her response, tapping the tips of his fingers together and flashing a smile.

"And if you survived? How would you feel then?"

"If I didn't die?" Spots of red flared on her cheeks.

"If you didn't die."

"I guess I'd feel relieved."

"Excellent," Dr. McCurl said. "So what we've learned is that a journey out onto the back porch will be excruciating. You'll be positive you're going to die. But you won't. I repeat, you won't. You'll survive." He sounded so confident, so step-by-step.

He took her hand and gently tugged her into the kitchen, reminding me of the trip she'd taken with Aunt Ruby a few months ago. Her hip caught every piece of furniture on the way, but nothing toppled, nothing was blocking her path. I could tell by the way she stumbled that her eyes were closed.

I remembered the afternoon when she'd actually gone out onto the porch on her own and done that spastic dance of fear. I didn't want to see that again.

"Take a deep breath, Mrs. Tedley. All the lovely summer smells."

"A meteorite landed in a backyard on Virginia Street several years ago and almost killed a two-year old." She sounded like a reporter announcing a natural disaster.

"Well, there's nothing in the sky today but white clouds."

"Someone planted a bomb in a Washington mailbox and when it exploded a piece of metal shot right through an innocent bystander's leg."

"Not a bomb in sight. Just marigolds and petunias."

"Eight student nurses were murdered in Chicago by a boy named Richard Speck." Her voice was rising.

"We are in Scarborough, Mrs. Tedley."

Mom running through her exotic repertoire of tragedies and Dr. McCurl singing the world's praises. They stayed on the porch for almost ten minutes. As they stepped back into the house, Mom tripped over the stoop. Had she kept her eyes closed? Did Dr. McCurl realize she hadn't seen the white clouds and the flowers he'd described so vividly? He kept congratulating her for being so brave, but I knew she kept imagining meteors and dead nurses the entire time.

When Dr. McCurl left, he took whatever victory there was along with him. At dinner that night, I urged Mom to talk about the experience but she refused. "I can't bear to remember," she pleaded. I hated seeing how relieved Dad was not to have to hear about her afternoon.

My father had erected a small lean-to in the centre of the Grey Bay lot plus an actual outhouse down near the road. He was talking non-stop about building a cabin sometime over the summer, if he could take a few weeks away from his part-time Texaco responsibilities.

I tried to understand how Grey Bay was an escape for him, a place where he could pretend nothing bad had ever happened, unless you counted Mom's refusal to leave the curtained-off back seat on her one and only trip there. The memory was a constant reminder, to me at least, that things were not at all right. But he could apparently pretend that he'd never had a heart attack. The trees had never heard Grammie's voice ordering them around. Aunt Ruby had never taken him behind a small cluster of beech trees and droned on about how worried she was about my mother's situation.

Wendy Fergie had never cast her eyes on Grey Bay and remarked what a dinky pond it was compared to the Atlantic Ocean. Aunt Veronica and Uncle Maurice had never had to lie and compliment him on his lean-to and outhouse when they were obviously finding the whole thing uncivilized. Lonny Milford had never pitied me for being forced to go along with such a dumb dream as my father's paradise.

I couldn't understand how he thought Grey Bay could solve his problems, our problems, with or without a cabin. To me, a trip there was a complicated kind of running away.

Dad and I were playing backyard golf, heading up the yard from hole seven to eight, when Mom's shaky shadow appeared at the screen door. She was having another of her fits, half-calling, half-crying, not making much sense.

"For Christ's sake, what's wrong now?"

He disappeared into the house. Abandoned, I swung out of turn, slamming the ball out of the yard. It landed in the driveway and bounced on the asphalt. I bounded after it. So did Queen Mary, shooting into action. She and I collided midway down the drive as the ball escaped between us and rolled under Lonny's shiny white Chev where it was parked on the street. Lonny was sitting in the driver's seat, twisting the steering wheel and making vroom, vroom noises. Lissy was sitting beside him.

Dad came out onto the front porch, shaking his head ominously. He strode down to the car and stopped by the driver's side.

"Where you headed?" he said.

Lonny blushed. "Nowhere," he said, his hands dropping off the wheel.

Dad nodded, as if he'd been there himself.

"So how's your dad?" he asked, apparently turning the conversation in a whole new direction.

"Not feeling so good these days." Lonny turned pale. "He has trouble breathing."

"That's a shame." Dad slapped his palm against the car roof. "So how have you been spending your summer?"

"Nothing much. Working part-time at Eli Lily. Hanging around."

"Driving nowhere," Dad said, his tone sharpening. "Hey, isn't that my daughter sitting there in the passenger seat?"

"Yep," Lonny answered, swallowing. "I'm just making her laugh."

"Lissy loves to laugh, that's a fact. But you mean to tell me you don't have anything better to do on this gorgeous summer evening than play cars with a retarded girl?"

"I'm killing some time," Lonny said.

"Sure," my father said. "Why not? But Mrs. Tedley and I don't like Lissy going somewhere we don't know about, even if it's nowhere with you. Now let her the hell out of there."

Lonny looked like he'd been kicked down a staircase. He stretched across Lissy and pushed open the passenger door.

"Go on now," he said. "The drive's over. Shoo."

Once Lissy was out on the sidewalk, Dad leaned down and practically stuck his face into Lonny's window.

"One more favour," he said. "Move your goddamn car. Our golf ball is underneath it."

Lonny drove clear to the end of the street and turned west on Maine Road. Dad watched until he was out of sight. Then he scuffed the ball away from the curb and kicked it hard toward me. "Next time you hit a ball out of the backyard, you lose," he said through tight lips.

★

Dr. McCurl arrived at two o'clock sharp, wearing a red bow tie and red suspenders. He was grinning ear to ear. He ignored my mother's nervous small talk and refused a glass of iced tea.

"Let's get right to work, Mrs. Tedley," he said, still grinning. "You did wonders with the living room window and the back porch. You'll do fine with this next threshold as well."

He was referring to the front door, gateway to Mars, Jupiter, Saturn and Uranus. He wanted my mother to stand in front of the propped-open screen door and breathe in the sour smell of baby crabapples, and, more importantly, to see and be seen.

Mom launched into her excuses, stressing Lissy's recent runaways.

"I picture her mangled and crying for help," she explained, holding onto the floor lamp by the couch. "My brain's like a horror movie."

"There's nothing horrible beyond that door, it's a perfectly normal suburban street."

Dr. McCurl was working to pry her fingers off the lamp as he spoke.

"The fears are deep inside your own head, Mrs. Tedley. You

have to stop externalizing."

"But my mother's lost somewhere in Europe. We haven't even heard from her. And my husband, I think he's working too hard again. Another heart attack could be the end of him."

"None of which is any of our concern at the moment," Dr. McCurl said flatly. "Let go of the lamp."

His fingers dug into hers until both their hands were red. Then he gave up and started pulling on her arms, dragging both her and the floor lamp toward the door. In the middle of the room, the lamp popped out of her hands and swung back and forth for a few seconds. By the time it had steadied itself, Dr. McCurl had Mom pulled to the front door where she clung to the frame, weeping.

I stole quietly to the front window, looking for something dreadful that might explain her awful crying. Several parked cars, Lonny's white Chevy among them, were steaming in the sun. I could see Queen Mary curled into a ball beneath the hedge. The Remington twins were sunbathing in their front yard on matching orange, pink and purple beach towels. A grey squirrel chased a half-bald black one across the Burrs' driveway. Finally, I saw one thing amiss: Mr. Milford, a living skeleton, sitting in a rickety deck chair on his front porch.

Did I think "skeleton" first, or did Mom? *Oh no,* I thought, *what if she thinks Mr. Milford looks like a skeleton?* I heard her say the word out loud and heave a huge sigh as she fell back into Dr. McCurl's arms.

"Did you see it?" she asked.

Dr. McCurl was pulling her to the couch. Her eyes were snapped open like bottle caps.

"See what?" he asked.

"The skeleton on the Milford porch."

"No nonsense, Mrs. Tedley. You saw an emaciated man, that's all." He kept reasoning with her until she stopped saying "skeleton" and agreed to go with sick man.

"It was a shock," she said.

"But now it's over and done. You survived, Mrs. Tedley."

He straightened his bow tie. "Next week, we'll take a short walk," he said.

As soon as Mom and I were alone, she started pacing back and forth between the couch and the easy chair. It looked as if she would throw herself down onto one of them, but she'd swivel at the last moment and head back across the room. I stepped in front of the chair. She stopped a few inches away as if I were a wall sprung up from nowhere then spun around and headed for the couch. She was making me feel as if I had no substance. I might as well have been invisible. I was less than a windowpane, less than wasted Mr. Milford.

"Fuck," I shouted. "Stop acting so crazy!" She didn't react, not so much as a twitch, so I left, shouting, "The bones are coming to get you" and letting the screen door slam.

*

Dear Robby,

The world is twice the size I thought it was. In fact, the Atlantic Ocean could swallow Lake Ontario in one gulp. I'm writing this in the back seat of our car. My Dad has parked next to a mailbox and is waiting for me to finish. Sometimes I feel like I've lost you. But I know you're out there. The Maritime provinces are beautiful, but nothing can take the place of our Valhalla Park.

XO   Wendy   XO

*

Dad and I spent the weekend together at Grey Bay. Uncle Frank was looking after Lissy until Sunday dinner, when he'd drive her back home. We were supposed to be home by six, but got held up in traffic, so didn't turn onto Arizona Avenue until almost eight. I remember Dad saying "Boy, your mother's going to give us hell," and thinking, *sure, if she's paying any attention,* just before we spotted the ambulance in our driveway and the police cruiser parked at the curb.

"What now?" Dad groaned. He slammed on the brakes right there in the middle of the street and leapt out of the car. Mr. Burr hurried over. He was wearing his cop uniform, which made me feel scared in a way the ambulance didn't. I stayed in the car, trying not to stare at any of the neighbours who were staring at my father.

He came back to the car, opened the passenger door and held out his hand. I had no choice but to take it and let him yank me out.

"What is it?" I said as we walked together toward the house.

"Don't worry, your mother's all right," he said. Of course she was all right, Dr. McCurl was always promising her that she would be: perfectly all right. Nothing could happen to my mother, wasn't that what everyone always said?

Another cop was standing in our living room along with a stranger. There was blood on one leg of his Bermuda shorts.

"Whose blood is that?" I asked. Nobody answered so I tried again. "Whose blood!"

"Shut up," Dad said, "Lissy's had an accident."

"What kind of an accident?"

"I said shut up," he repeated, pushing past me.

"Take it easy, kid," the cop said. "Everything's going to be okay."

"But what happened?"

He looked at me, sizing me up, then placed his hands on my shoulders. "Someone tried to molest your sister in the schoolyard. Do you know what that means?" When I nodded, he continued. "A couple of teenaged boys. But your sister fought like a tiger. This man here was walking along Kingston Road when he heard her scream. He got to her before things went too far." The cop was watching me as if I might go off like a firecracker at any moment. "She's going to be okay, okay? The ambulance is going to take her to the hospital so the doctors can make sure she doesn't have any broken bones."

He had been holding my shoulders very gently, but now he let go. I could still feel the pressure of his hands. I stayed beside him, watching as the ambulance attendants carried Lissy out of her bedroom on a stretcher. She seemed to be enjoying the attention. She didn't seem the least bit upset.

Dad was standing in his bedroom doorway. His back was to me, but I could hear him snuffling. Mom was scrunched up in a corner of the bed, sitting on one of the pillows, the back of her head pressed to the wall. She was talking to herself, pure gibberish, like Lissy when she gets upset, snot dripping off the tip of her nose. Dad was crying. I felt a flash of rage at everyone in the fucking house, rage even at Lissy, whose not knowing any better gave her an excuse for every stupid thing she did. But there was no excuse for her going alone to Emergency.

I turned away and went to my own room and threw myself onto the bed. Which of us was the most responsible for this mess? Dad should have realized that a day of outings with Uncle Frank would have made Lissy too high to settle. Mom couldn't take care of a flea let alone a retarded daughter. *If anything bad happens to our girl.* Christ, it was Grammie's fault for taking her resentment off to Europe. What a jerk I was, for believing anyone who had ever used the word *okay*.

*

When I woke up next morning, the bedroom door down the hall was still shut tight. I expected to find a note on the kitchen table, explaining that, because of recent circumstances, neither parent would be getting out of bed for a long, long time. I poured a bowl of Cheerios and drank half a pitcher of cherry Kool-Aid. I fed Queen Mary and combed my hair. The street was still asleep as I wheeled my bike up the driveway. I rode the five miles to East General Hospital, dodging buses and bucking potholes. It felt good to pedal, my heart pumping so powerfully in my chest that it seemed my ribs were shaking. The front lobby was huge and confusing, with signs pointing to Cardiology, Admitting, Surgery, words I couldn't match up with Lissy, almost molested. Then I saw a smaller sign: Information Desk. I asked for Melissa Tedley. The clerk said something about psychiatry and visiting hours, but I registered the room number, 302, took an elevator and followed more signs.

Lissy was in a room all by herself. She seemed drugged, her wrists and ankles tied together with leather straps. Was this normal? I thought about untying her, sneaking her out of there, but where could I take her that was safe? Aunt Ruby and Uncle Frank had blown it, and Aunt Veronica was a shopper, not a guardian.

"Excuse me. Visiting hours aren't until two o'clock."

A heavy-set, middle-aged nurse, probably capable of carrying me to the nearest exit, was standing in the doorway.

"Why did you tie her up?"

"Because she was trying to run away."

All right. Finally. Someone to give me straight answers.

"What does it mean to be almost molested?" I asked.

"I'm sorry, but who are you in relation to the patient?"

"Her brother."

For a second I thought she was going to hug me. "Do you know what rape means?" she asked gently.

"Yeah."

"What?"

"Someone forcing someone else to have sex." I was thinking back to Aunt Ruby's birds and bees talk a few years ago. A thought came and went about me getting a boner while dancing with Wendy at her birthday party in April.

"Your sister was almost raped. Do you understand?"

"A man from Kingston Road stopped them." I wished I'd taken a better look at him. I couldn't tell the difference between him and the would-be rapist and that made me feel nauseous.

"Terrible things can happen when a child like your sister wanders away from home." She seemed to see something in the way I was looking or standing. "Are you going to be okay?" she asked.

"I'm not sure," I said, "but I'm trying."

She let me stay in the room with Lissy. I stood beside her bed for at least an hour, watching her sleep and wondering who'd be the next Tedley to end up in hospital.

*

Dad was on the phone to Aunt Ruby when a couple of detectives showed up at our door. The older one was on the beefy side and wore a loud checked sports coat.

"I wonder if we might ask you a few questions," he said, holding his badge out for inspection. Dad put his hand up like an invisible Stop sign.

"I'm in the middle of a phone call," he said. He'd been crying.

"Perhaps your wife…"

Mom hadn't budged from her bed since Sunday night. "Indisposed," said Dad.

"We need only a few minutes of your time," the detective insisted, polite but pushy.

"Talk to him," Dad said, pointing at me. He gave me a small shove forward as he headed back to the kitchen.

The young cop looked a little like Lonny Milford, but cleaned up. His brush cut made his elephant ears stand out. He was definitely not pleased to be talking to a kid, but decided to make the most of it.

"How often does your sister take off?" he asked me.

"Every chance she gets," I answered.

"Ever follow her?"

"All the time. I'm the one who always brings her back."

"How often does she go to the schoolyard?" The older cop leaned in closer, his nostrils flaring.

"A lot. It's her favourite place."

"Does anyone else hang out there?"

I explained about the high school kids, making sure I called them hoods.

"But I don't think any of them would ever try to rape her," I said. "It was probably Lonny Milford."

The moment I said his name, I felt enormous power. I told them how he knocked the milk carton out of my hands and split my lip, but not about the shit attack. I told them how Dad had found Lissy in the passenger seat of Lonny's Chevy and said that his father was dying, just to give the picture of Lonny's juvenile delinquency an extra touch.

The detectives asked me to repeat a few things. I was doing some serious embellishing, good for filling several pages of their notebooks.

"Lonny was the one who raped my sister," I finished. "He wrecked my family. My mother wasn't even afraid until she met him. My father had a heart attack from just having to live across the street from him."

"Don't you worry, we'll check everything out," the young detective said. The old guy snapped his notebook shut. They seemed relieved to be finished with me.

"It's the way I feel," I said from the porch as they headed back to their car, but I don't think they heard me.

★

Dr. McCurl arrived the next day wearing a pair of white running shoes. He was clearly still planning on taking my mother for a walk. Aunt Ruby met him at the front door and related the whole story of Sunday night's accident. She didn't say much about Lissy, but concentrated on Mom, as if she'd been the one molested.

Once he'd been thoroughly briefed, she led Dr. McCurl into the bedroom, where Mom was huddled on the bed, a pink and platinum blonde lump. It looked as though she had shut down some engine deep inside her body.

"Mrs. Tedley. Mrs. Tedley!" Dr. McCurl shouted. "You can hear me. Of course you can hear me. The world goes on whether you acknowledge it or not." He paused to study her more closely.

When he brushed her forehead with his fingers, she drew back further into the pillow. The silence that followed made me very uncomfortable. I decided to share my detective story with Dr. McCurl, thinking it might make my mother feel better as well.

"I told them who to look for," I stated, "so pretty soon they'll catch him and the neighbourhood will be safe again."

Aunt Ruby patted me lightly on the head, but Dr. McCurl frowned. He turned away and continued talking, this time more softly, to Mom. No way was she going for a walk, everyone could see that, but some progress had to be made, some tiny step. He asked her to open her eyes and look at him for ten seconds. On the first count there was no response, so he reminded her of their deal, their agreement to accomplish something new every week.

"Open your eyes, Mrs. Tedley, and that will be it for today."

He started counting again, *one, two*. Finally, Mom opened her eyes, staring into Dr. McCurl's eyes and holding it for a count of ten, proving that she'd heard everything.

Dr. McCurl whispered, "Good," and laid his hand on her forehead. "That's progress," he said, turning to Aunt Ruby. "We may have to consider hospitalization, but let's take it day by day for now. And perhaps a little medication would help to smooth the rough edges."

He walked past me without so much as a nod. Perhaps I wasn't as invisible to Dr. McCurl as I was to my mother, just completely irrelevant.

*

Mr. Milford died the next day. Neighbours gathered along the front walk like people at a parade, bowing their heads as the ambulance guys wheeled the body away. Our second ambulance in less than a week. We were a universe falling apart.

Mr. Milford was only a shape under a sheet. I was reminded of the wintry night when Dad was carted out of the house on a stretcher, a sheet tucked right up to his chin. He was a neck and a skull away from being dead. At this very moment, Mom's fears made some sense. Lonny trailed behind the stretcher, hardly able to lift his feet. He ducked into the ambulance beside the body. Aunt Ruby said the police had already questioned him, said he'd spent all Sunday evening by his father's bedside. But they were planning to talk to him again after the funeral, she added. I didn't think Lonny would ever come back to Arizona Avenue. His father had been the only thing between him and oblivion.

"I think we're over the worst of it," Aunt Ruby said, once the ambulance had gone and the neighbours had scattered to their separate houses. "We'll soon be back to normal."

*

Dear Folks,

Amsterdam was an eye-opener. Polluted canals and prostitutes who do their business in store windows. Brussels was full of gargoyles and old churches as cold as tombs. I've just arrived in Paris. The people are barely civil. I'm having a good time. I'm being educated, right, left and centre. You should be ashamed of yourselves, hiding out in suburbia, letting the world pass you by.

Grammie

EIGHT

MR. MILFORD'S SERVICE at McDougall & Brown Funeral Home was damped down with heavy organ music. I'd only ever seen one dead body, my Dad's Great Uncle Luke, back before I started kindergarten. I'd been lifted into someone's arms to look into the open casket, and wondered what he was doing there, fast asleep in a wooden box in a roomful of visitors. Mr. Milford looked a long way from sleep. He reminded me of a store mannequin, with his face powdery pink and his lips as bright as if he'd been eating strawberries. The preacher asked us to imagine people in paradise gathering around the pearly gates to welcome Mr. Milford in. I pictured Eaton's Christmas windows where mannequins were dressed up like elves.

The room reminded me of a fancy parlour on *The Secret Storm*, with its pictures of green hills and placid lakes. There were heaps of hot-coloured flowers, including a jungle-like arrangement of yellow lilies on top of the casket's bottom half. Relatives who'd never set foot on Arizona Avenue while Mr. Milford was alive, neighbours, co-workers and Lonny's few scummy friends—everyone sort of drifted to the middle of the room as if they'd all had the same thought, that there would be the only safe place should the funeral parlour suddenly start to sag and heave. Lonny was alone in one corner, wet-eyed and pale. He was hunched over, chain-smoking, a cloud of grey smoke separating him from everyone else. Was this really the pervert who had molested Lissy?

"Unlucky bastard," my father muttered. At first I thought he meant Lonny, but now I'm not sure. It crossed my mind that everyone in the room was probably afraid—of death, of ghosts, of waking up in hell. My mother would have felt right at home. But poor dead Mr. Milford wasn't really very scary. It was the shadows under my father's eyes that drew an icicle up and down my spine.

*

Before Dad and I brought Lissy home from East General a young-looking doctor talked to us about how important it was to keep her occupied, suggesting a job at a sheltered workshop where mentally retarded workers put nuts on bolts or stamps on envelopes, that sort of stuff. Dad nodded, but I knew he was just being polite. That they were actually letting Lissy come home at all, considering what I'd told those detectives, was a miracle.

"Home?" Lissy asked when she saw our car. Dad handed her a Sweet Marie bar.

"Home it is," he said, "and then maybe we'll head up to Grey Bay for a nice long holiday."

"No way," I said. "Mom can't even get out of bed."

"She'll come around."

"But we can't go anywhere until she's able to take care of herself."

He banged the heel of his hand on the steering wheel. "Bloody hell, Robby. You're like the voice of doom."

"She can't stay alone," I said quietly. I couldn't believe this.

"So you stay with her then," he sneered. "Mr. Take Care of Everything."

*

Next morning Dad started packing the Valiant with toolboxes, coolers and grocery bags. I sat to one side, my legs dangling over the door to the crawl space beneath the porch, watching him come and go. When he was finally empty-handed, he turned and asked me ever so politely to follow him.

I rose slowly and did what I was told, letting the screen door bang behind me. He led me through the kitchen, down the hall and into the bedroom where Mom was propped up in bed like a dying heroine in an old movie. Her platinum blonde do had turned dark at the roots.

"Your mother's feeling better," Dad said. "So now's a good time for me to get some stuff done at Grey Bay. And two weeks of running free will be good for Lissy."

"You have to take care of your heart," Mom mumbled, her voice shaky but trying for a lilt.

"It's healthy to be outdoors and break a sweat." Dad took a deep breath, exhaling in a thin, controlled stream. "I'll be fine."

"Do you mind terribly, Robby?" Mom asked.

"Staying behind," Dad added.

"If Ruby hadn't gone partners with you at the Texaco..." Mom said, trailing off, not waiting for my answer.

"We've been over this, Flo. Ruby's going to have to work her tail off. August's a busy month. Anyway, what would a fourteen-year-old boy do in the middle of nowhere? Looking after you can be his summer job."

Was he really okay with leaving me behind with Mom? Could he actually get away with this? Was it even legal? Dr. McCurl was on holiday for the next couple of weeks. Everyone was in the process of leaving or had left already.

"I won't be any trouble," Mom said. Every word she uttered had that trace of forced melody to it. "I can get out of bed when I need to. And Ruby will drop by every day for a bit. Isn't that right, Ed?"

"No trouble at all," my father said. "Understand, Robby? You do what you can for your mother. Any time of day, whatever she wants."

I took hold of the sharpest part of my anger and aimed it right at Dad's throat. "Yeah, okay," I said, making it clear that it wasn't.

"Come on now, Robby. Like I said, Flo, he'd rather stay home, hang out with friends, do all that teenager stuff."

"I can hardly remember being a teenager," Mom sang dreamily.

"Don't bother getting out of bed." Dad kissed her on the forehead, then the lips. "Love you. Don't you forget it. You're my sweetie pie, no matter what."

"Bye bye." She waved, smiling.

We walked out to the driveway. Dad passed me a big wad of bills, enough for at least a couple of weeks, he said. Lissy was already in the car.

"I was fourteen once and miserable all the time," he said, leaning over and kissing me on the top of my head. Then he and Lissy drove away, disappeared around the corner. Gone. I looked at each of the houses across the street to see if anyone had observed how I'd been abandoned, but there wasn't a single sign of human presence anywhere. The street was like a ghost town in an old western. It spooked me to be standing in the driveway alone. If ever there were a perfect time for the sky to fall, this would be it.

★

Another breakfast in bed for my mother: her usual cereal and toast. She smiled, babbling about the wonderful weather and how much fun my father and Lissy must be having up at the Bay. Running out of small talk, she said something about getting up later, getting back in the swing of things, but we both knew that the only getting up she'd actually be doing would be for trips to the bathroom.

Lunch in bed as well, Campbell's green pea soup and a grilled cheese sandwich. Other days we had golden mushroom or cream of tomato, with either a tuna or bologna sandwich. Each time I brought in her tray, I had to stop myself from tipping it onto her.

Aunt Ruby arrived each evening at six, waltzing into the house, her earrings jangling, carrying some takeout meal—Harvey's hamburgers and chocolate milkshakes, for instance—straight to the bedroom. Last night it was pepperoni pizza, the two of them spilling crumbs on the sheets. The night before that we'd had Chopsticks Chinese. She brought news to keep Mom entertained, all sorts of tidbits about her swell day at the Texaco, about Uncle Frank's latest gig at a small country and western club recently opened in Etobicoke, a movie she saw the night before, even a story about Aunt Veronica spilling a strawberry daiquiri on one of Uncle Maurice's city hall friends. When she was all talked out, she painted my mother's fingernails pink.

Despite my father's notion of me hanging out with friends, I was spending most of my time at home. Marco was often busy with family stuff anyway, and Louie Burr was at a camp up at Wasaga Beach. I watched TV with Mom, sitting beside her on the bed, hours and hours of reruns: *Red Skelton*, *The Avengers*, *Love on a Rooftop*, *It Takes a Thief* and *The FBI*. One night we watched *To Tell the Truth*. We were supposed to be guessing which one of three chubby middle-aged men had been Marilyn Monroe's bodyguard, but I wasn't in the mood. I was feeling really weird and worked up, worried that something terrible was going to happen. I tried pinching myself. A couple of times I banged my head against the headboard. Finally, I got off the bed and paced the hall, trying to rid my mind of images of my father and Lissy floating face down in Grey Bay. The craziness went on like this for quite a while. I fought it until I couldn't fight anymore. Through the door to the bedroom I could see the side of Mom's face with her one eye staring at the TV. She looked like a zombie. She hadn't even realized that I'd left the room.

One day she'll die, I thought, lying in bed like that, too stunned to take another breath.

So much anger was flowing through me, I thought if I touched anything glass or porcelain, I'd break it in two. I kicked the living room hassock. I knocked over the velour chair. I picked up one of the oversized cushions on the couch and threw it into the dining room, grabbed another and threw it into the front hall. Still the mad energy kept building. I flung open the hall closet and swatted hangers back and forth along the rail. That made a satisfying screech and jangle. Then I spotted Mom's accordion. I opened the snaps and lifted it from its case. It weighed a ton, but I managed to hoist it up with the straps on my shoulders and stumbled with it back into the bedroom.

The Jolly Green Giant was grinning at a bunch of baby peas and carrots that danced around his feet. Fuck the Jolly Green Giant. Running my fingers back and forth over the keyboard and thumping the bass buttons with a fist, I drowned the Giant's jingle in awful noise, every imaginable discord.

I stood between my shocked mother and the TV and played until she clapped her hands over her ears. I played until she dragged the covers up over her head. I played through the final five minutes of *To Tell the Truth*, a Swanson Frozen TV Dinner commercial, a Marlborough ad and a preview of new fall shows. I played until she ripped off the covers and reared up on the bed, trying to wrench the accordion away. We ended up in a heap, me sprawled across the open bellows, breathing heavily, she hanging over the edge of the mattress, like clinging to a sinking ship.

"Why are you torturing me?" she gasped. She crawled back up to the head of the bed, careful not to touch me.

I didn't know what to say. Why was I so angry anyway?

"You're scaring me, Robby."

I wanted to say that since she was afraid of everything else, why not be afraid of me as well, but I couldn't make the words in my mouth. All I could utter was babble. I might have been Lissy. I shook my head back and forth as if trying to dislodge something stuck in my brain.

"I'm sorry," I said finally, moving over to Dad's side of the bed, where I wouldn't block the TV. *The Wild Wild West* was on now, a train robbery in progress. She shrunk away from me, into the corner of the room. We didn't exchange another word until the news came on and Mom asked me politely to change the channel.

*

The next night, Marco and I went on a rampage. We didn't talk much about it. I simply suggested that we mess things up at the variety store. Marco could always be counted on for some chaos. Together, we were perilous, men from *U.N.C.L.E.* gone bad.

The storeowner, a wiry Japanese guy with a big head, always scowled at Lissy, refusing to take coins from her hands. He'd flinch from her touch as if she had leprosy. That night, we paid him back. Marco distracted him by fingering the front-counter candy, while I grabbed an armful of *Playboy* magazines and spread them, centrefold open, on various shelves, propped up against the canned goods, between loaves of bread, behind the pet food. When I ran out of magazines, I goosed everything soft, leaving prints in packages of hot dog buns, bags of marshmallows, boxes of Kleenex, Twinkies.

We moved on to the schoolyard where Marco and I had been treated like kids for years. We hit it hard, tying the swings up into metal knots, digging heel holes in the baseball diamond, tipping over the slide.

On the way back to Arizona Avenue, we fell into hedges, stamped through flower beds and threw stones at yappy dogs. Revenge on all the old women who'd ever ordered us off their front lawns, on all the fathers in undershirts who didn't want us anywhere near their daughters, on all the terriers and spaniels who'd tried to sink their teeth into our shins.

We were back home by eleven thirty, not satisfied. We tiptoed up the Burrs' driveway and turned their hose on full blast.

"Fucking cop," I whispered to Marco.

At the Remingtons' lawn he yanked out clumps of petunias and marigolds.

"Fucking Jehovah's Witnesses," he said.

Finally, worn out, I kicked in one of Lonny's basement windows.

"Fucking death," I said.

Marco gave me a worried look.

Wrecked and wasted, we stretched out on the grass behind the lilac bushes in my backyard and stared up at the stars. They made me feel dangerously small.

"I'd like to fill the Texaco gas pumps with pork and beans and make all the cars in Scarborough fart like crazy."

"I'd like to turn my Uncle Pasquale's homemade wine into rocket fuel. So long, Uncle."

"I'd like to appoint my Uncle Maurice alderman of Siberia. My cousin Roma could be a Siberian husky."

"I'd like to send my cousin Maria to Africa. She's big enough to feed a whole tribe of cannibals."

"I'd like to switch brains with my sister."

"I'd like to fuck my sister when she's fast asleep."

I looked at Marco. Jesus. But what the hell, he had his reasons. My most secret wish that night was to drag my mother out of the house and into the schoolyard, tie her to a swing and push her so high she'd smash a hole in the sky and catapult through it, never to be afraid of anything again.

★

Next day, instead of serving Mom breakfast in bed, I set a place for her at the kitchen table. I called out to let her know I'd already poured the milk on her Shredded Wheat. Let her refuse to budge: I could be every bit as stubborn. Three hours later I served the soggy cereal to Queen Mary, who lapped up the milk and turned up her nose at the rest.

At lunchtime I put a bowl of tomato soup and a grilled cheese sandwich at my mother's place at the table.

"Lunch is ready," I yelled, digging into my own. Her soup cooled, her sandwich grew rubbery.

I hung around outside with Louie and Dana for most of the afternoon, taking turns doing slap shots against the school with a rubber ball. When I returned, the soup and the sandwich were gone. Aunt Ruby arrived, balancing a pizza carton. I played it cool. "Mom eats in here now," I said. Aunt Ruby looked suspicious, but I didn't back down. I took the pizza from her and set it down in the middle of the table. "Pizza," I called.

When Mom failed to appear, Aunt Ruby said, "Maybe she's not up to it, Robby. Maybe she'd rather we bring her a slice or two."

"She's likely taking a nap," I said, keeping my eyes steady. "She'll be hungry when she wakes up."

Warily, Aunt Ruby agreed to put several slices in the oven to keep them warm. The whole house soon smelled like fresh-baked pizza. She apologized for having to eat and run, but Uncle Frank was singing out in Hamilton.

"You're amazing," she said, giving me a hug.

After washing the dishes I breezed into Mom's bedroom without even looking at her, unplugged the TV set as *The Beverly Hillbillies* theme song began and carried it back to its proper place in the living room. I watched Jethro Clampitt try to coax a pig out of Miss Hathaway's file drawers. Just beyond the borders of the television screen, I caught a glimpse of Mom's white nightgown drifting into the kitchen. I heard the creak of the oven door, followed by a clatter of plates and the jingle of cutlery. She came into the hall with a plate of pizza slices, her shoulders hunched, her head bent low. The look she gave me would have sent Jethro scurrying for the hills.

I felt lightheaded, though scoured by that glance, but in a good way. My plan had worked. Sure, she was mad at me, but anger was preferable to fear. Anger got her out of bed and into the kitchen. Anger gave legs to hunger. Anger was the engine that would finally drive her back out into the world, a positive force if aimed right.

★

Eventually Mom was taking all three meals sitting across from me at the kitchen table. If she wanted to watch TV, she sat beside me on the living room sofa. On the ninth day, she went down to the rec room for a while. I could hear the murmur of the basement TV through the floorboards. With my help, she was even making her bed in the mornings, then lying on top of the covers if she needed an afternoon nap.

At lunch on day ten, I was feeling pretty good about things, even though we weren't really talking to one another and I'd had no word from Dad. Actually, I was feeling pretty good about myself and how much I'd managed to accomplish. I thought of Dr. McCurl with his stern and confident way of speaking. I'd been so successful in moving my mother from bedroom to kitchen to living room, so why not give the back porch a try? Or the front door? Maybe I'd be the one to take her for a walk around the block. I pictured Dad's face as he arrived home to find Mom standing on the front walk, waiting to welcome him and Lissy with giant hugs.

"I've been thinking," I said, just as she was ready to take a bite of her salmon sandwich. The sudden sound of my voice startled her and she dropped it back onto the plate.

I did my best to soften my tone, make it sound gentle, persuasive. "Maybe it's time we started thinking about going outside again. Like Dr. McCurl said."

"You're not my doctor," she said, enunciating every syllable.

I closed my eyes for a second. Dr. McCurl stuck to the details at hand, I remembered, putting all his focus on getting my mother to do exactly what he wanted. He simply told her what the plan was then went about making it happen.

"Your doctor already prescribed a trip to the back porch," I said, keeping a neutral expression. "It's like being told to take a pill. The doctor just tells you once. It's up to you to continue taking that pill every day."

She was staring at me. At first I thought she was maybe trying to figure out whether I was being serious or playing some kind of a game, but then I realized that her eyes were actually looking through me into some other world where I suppose the worst had already happened.

How could I explain that I was trying to rescue her. If she were about to fall off a cliff, wouldn't I do everything I could to reach out and grab her before she did? If she were tied to the railroad tracks, wouldn't I tear at the knots until my fingers were bloody and whisk her off to safety at the last minute?

"It's going to be okay," I promised. Never mind whether she was listening or not. I needed a plan.

*

I ate breakfast slowly the next morning. I didn't have much of an appetite, just had half a bowl of Rice Krispies and a few spoonfuls of hard honey. Mom didn't show up. After brushing my teeth and getting dressed, I found her still in bed. Her eyes were open, but she closed them the second I entered her room. The lump in my throat made my words sound as if they'd been squeezed through a straw to get out.

"Come on," I said. "We've got things to do today."

I leaned over and tried to lift her. She bore down. Instead of struggling, I picked up her legs and swung them over the edge of the bed. Her upper torso slid forwards and I was able to pull her into a standing position.

"Good job," I said. Once up, she let me lead her from the bedroom to the kitchen.

"Do you want something to eat? Maybe some eggs?"

I opened the fridge door and bent over to take a look at the things on the shelves. I said I'd be happy to scramble eggs for her once we'd made some *progress*, as Dr. McCurl called it. I took her by the elbow and steered her to the back door. She took a few steps, willingly enough, then abruptly began to push against me.

In my efforts to keep her moving straight to the back door, I pushed her face too hard into the screen. Rows of tiny red squares were bright on her right cheek when she regained her balance. "Sorry," I said, but her cry drowned out the apology. It took a bit of complicated footwork to get the screen door open, then the outside door as well, but I managed, pushing her ahead of me. I didn't mean to be so violent, but she had to realize that once she'd faced the terror we'd all be free again.

We fell out onto the back porch together, tumbling to our knees like some kind of clumsy four-legged beast. She turned and poked her fingers at my face, begging me to quit. She was crying non-stop now.

I was crying a little myself, but it never crossed my mind to stop. I had to keep going, to pull her down the porch steps onto the patio then out into the yard. I wanted to remove all her fears in one magnificent swoop. But then I recalled Dr. McCurl, how he was always talking to her about small steps.

"We're going back inside now," I said, stroking her cheek.

She clambered up off her knees and sped through the door, across the kitchen into the dining room and down the hall to her bedroom, slamming the door.

She'd done a brave thing and had earned a break. I stood outside the bedroom and called out, "Good job, Mom." I listened for a response. Nothing. "Mom?"

Then the doorbell chimed. Marco was standing on the porch. "I spotted the Remington twins sunbathing in their backyard," Marco said. "Why don't we go ask them to show us their tits."

I was still panting a little. I could hear Mom dragging her dresser across the bedroom to barricade the door.

Tits were the last thing on my mind, but I couldn't think of anything clever to send Marco away without noticing how upset I was. I let myself be persuaded.

Franny and Lucy were stretched out on the grass, wearing tinted granny glasses and matching purple bikinis. Their breasts were Barbie doll perfect and much bigger than they had seemed the previous summer whenever I ran into them at the Kingston Road Public Pool.

Marco was a dork. He disgraced himself with several cheap tit jokes, had his hands slapped several times and was quickly running out of stupid euphemisms, melons, beach balls and full moons.

"Come on, why won't you let me have a feel. I won't burst your balloons."

He got down on one knee and pretended to beg, his tongue hanging out the side of his mouth. Usually, Marco's dorkiness was a minor irritation, a mosquito bite, but that morning he was so stupid, I wished I had a bolt of lightning to throw, to send whatever brain he had in his sorry head up in smoke. But Franny and Lucy kept bursting into giggles.

"You're acting like a ten-year-old," I said. "You all are."

"Screw you," Franny said, not very Jehovah's Witness–like. "Why don't you show us your dick?"

"Happy to."

The twins glanced at one another. Marco's mouth fell open. I thought about Wendy Fergie, but the excitement of showing myself at that moment and the disdain I felt for how juvenile the twins and Marco were being was more intense than anything I'd ever felt for Wendy.

"Under the weeping willow," Franny said. "Show us your dick over there."

"And then you'll show your tits. Share and share alike."

Franny nodded, which made Lucy nod as well. I was the first one under the willow, ducking beneath the long, low, whip-like branches that slapped at my arms and legs. It was a perfect hiding place. Not so long ago I'd hid there in a game of war, lying on my belly, my stick rifle ready to blast anyone who came too close.

Franny and Lucy stood right in front of me, Marco behind them. I started to undress. I could feel terror in the pit of my stomach, but no way was I surrendering to any kind of fear. I let my shorts drop, my underpants so white in the shadows they seemed to be glowing. I pulled them down past my knees. No one said a word. I had a bit of a boner. I'd never had a boner in front of anyone in my entire life, not even when Louie Burr and I were little kids and used to run around naked in his backyard. It got bigger, like those time-lapse photographs of flowers Miss Luther used to show us, a bud turning into a rose in seconds flat.

"Now it's your turn," I said, looking at one twin, then the other.

"Jesus," Marco whispered.

Franny lifted her bikini top away from her breasts, letting them tumble out. Lucy took the long way, undoing hers from the back, sliding it down her arms, her breasts squeezing together like they were going to burst. We stood there, staring at one another, Marco practically drooling, fumbling with the clasp on his shorts.

"Keep your pants on, Morelli," Franny said, eyes still fixed on me.

It was surprising what raced through my head. I thought about how girls' nipples looked like goosebumps. I thought about walking around naked with a boner for the rest of my life. I thought of Lissy, how she was almost raped. I thought about molesting the Remington twins. I thought about beating the crap out of Marco for his constant dorkiness.

And I thought about my mother, cowering in her bedroom, how much more afraid she'd be if she could see me now.

Franny and Lucy had already started covering up, giggling again like babies. Marco was back to balloons and adding pricks and sticks and wicks, just about anything that rhymed with dick. This had been nothing but a silly game for them.

"Fuck you," I said, suddenly feeling more exposed. I pulled up my underpants and shorts. "Marco's got a tiny dick," I sneered. "And the both of you have ugly nipples."

I ducked out from under the willow and headed home. Not one of them tried to stop me or shouted anything mean. They would probably spend the rest of the afternoon trying to figure me out.

Once home I couldn't settle down. I looked out the living room window a few times to see if Marco was coming to check up on me, but the street was empty. I slammed around the kitchen for a while, sending a few pot lids skimming across the floor, banging cupboard doors. Finally, I tried my mother's bedroom door. She was probably sitting on the edge of her bed, staring at phantoms like the Ghost of Christmas Past or the Headless Horseman.

"Don't be scared," I called through the door. "You've got to stop being so scared."

If I pushed in careful increments I could move the dresser bit by bit. I finally squeezed through and reached out for her, but she clawed her fingers across my face. I snatched one of the summer nightgowns that was folded on top of her chair and climbed up onto the bed with it. I pulled her arms back and tied them together at her wrists so she couldn't claw me again. She was moaning, trying to shake free, but I held on. When the knots were good and tight, I jumped off the bed, grabbed her under the arms and hefted her to a standing position. Her knees gave way a couple of times. It took all my strength to prop her up.

A part of me couldn't believe what I was doing. If I'd let myself pause for even a second, I would have lost my nerve. It was the fear that kept me going. The fear that was slowly destroying her from inside was driving me now.

We staggered all the way to the front hall where I forced her forehead against the screen.

"Tell me what you see."

I had to make sure her eyes were open, that she was actually looking at something other than the horrors inside her own head. I knew how she'd managed to fool Dr. McCurl by keeping her eyes shut. I had to do better.

"A tree," she whispered.

"A tree. Nothing to be afraid of. What else?"

She was whimpering. The back of her neck glistened with sweat.

"I don't know," she said. "The street."

"Nothing scary there. Just a street."

"It's what I feel, Robby," she gasped, "not what I see."

"So go ahead and feel. There's nothing wrong with feelings."

Her whimpers grew louder. "The mailman," she cried. "He's heading this way."

I knew the mailman would never understand what was going on. He didn't live in our world. I yanked Mom back into the living room and untied the nightgown from around her wrists. The instant she was free, she hit me on the chin, really clobbered me, then took off for her bedroom.

I stood there waiting for at least five minutes. There was no sign of the mailman anywhere on the street. The mailman had been a lie. Despite her terror, she had managed to trick me into letting her go. Wasn't this a kind of progress? I could see Dr. McCurl shaking my hand, congratulating me on accomplishing so much in less than two weeks.

I really wanted to tell Aunt Ruby all about Mom's progress when she arrived with vegetarian lasagna from Luigi's a few hours later. She of all people knew how elusive Mom could be. But I chickened out, simply saying that it had been a hard day.

"Where did you get those scratches on your face?" she asked.

"Some friends and I were playing under a willow tree."

"Do you think I should call the number Dr. McCurl gave me in case things got worse?" she asked. "Maybe she needs to be hospitalized. Maybe it's gone too far."

A wave of vertigo almost knocked me over, then another. I must have looked sick because Aunt Ruby was suddenly all over me, checking my forehead for fever, putting an arm around me, pulling me close.

It was making sense why Mom hadn't told Aunt Ruby about the evening I went a little crazy with the accordion, or my warning that today was the day I was going to insist that she go outside. She knew that without me, she'd be forced to leave the house for a long time. If Arizona Avenue was a scary place, imagine the mental hospital.

Aunt Ruby insisted on checking in on Mom. Well, so what, I thought. Either it was over or my mother would put on some kind of a performance to make sure she wasn't tossed into a padded cell. I didn't have the strength to worry any more.

I didn't follow Aunt Ruby into the bedroom, but I heard them talking. I heard Mom say she'd been trying to push herself a little more each day and had hit a temporary wall. Aunt Ruby asked if she had the energy to eat a piece of lasagna.

She and Mom ended up having their dinner in the bedroom. I turned on the TV and drowned out everything but the murmur of occasional conversation. Finally, there was nothing but quiet and Aunt Ruby came tip-toeing into the living room.

"She's exhausted, poor dear," she said, leaning over and kissing me on the cheek. "I suggested that she take a few days off, stay in bed."

I nodded at Aunt Ruby and let her coax a smile from me as well.

"You're something special, kiddo," she said as she was leaving. "I don't know how you manage to keep it all together."

For a moment, I almost gave in to a deep longing to tell the truth. But I could see how important it was to Aunt Ruby for me to be special. She was as lost as the rest of us and needed something or someone to pin her hopes on. Me? I wasn't feeling so special. My mother was not just scared of the outside now, she was scared of me.

*

Next morning, I couldn't find Mom. She wasn't in her bed or hiding inside her closet behind the plastic bags where she stored her winter clothes. No sign of her in the kitchen. I was having a hard time breathing. I checked the hall closet and underneath the basement stairs. I could hear myself gasp every time I took in air. She wasn't behind the furnace. I checked the backyard, but nothing had changed out there. A few more roses in bloom and a whole cloud of honeybees buzzing around the marigolds. I stared at the marigolds for a good ten minutes, with no clue what to do next.

I poured myself a glass of juice and sat down at the kitchen table. I wasn't sure whether the chair was trying to tip over or whether there was something wrong with my balance. My goal was to think logically. Wasn't it impossible for Mom to have walked away?

The shakiness in my stomach changed to nausea. I must have searched the house at least fifteen times. I looked everywhere I could think of, then sat down again and closed my eyes, hoping she would reappear when I opened them again. I started thinking crazy thoughts. Maybe someone had kidnapped her in a curtained car. Maybe Dad had arrived in the middle of the night and whisked her away somewhere where she'd be safe from me. Maybe the Costellos were giving her shelter and booze. Or maybe Lonny Milford stole her so that she could look after him, now that his father was dead. Maybe she never existed, maybe I'd made her up. It was the hour for *The Secret Storm*, so I flopped down on the couch, hoping to find her somewhere in the plot, sharing her suffering with the other characters.

She was gone: it was a fact. Where hardly mattered. Her absence was my fault entirely. It was like I had killed her yesterday. What kind of a monster destroys his own mother, claiming that he is trying to save her? When Aunt Ruby's car coasted into the driveway at dinner time, I didn't know what else to do but close my parent's bedroom door and tell her that Mom had taken her advice and spent most of the day napping on and off. When she hugged me goodbye, I was afraid I would shatter in her arms.

I slept in Mom's bed, in case she tried to sneak home in the middle of the night. But I woke up next morning still alone. My father and Lissy would be home the next day with their goddamned sunburns and dirty laundry. What would I say?

I started searching again. In the front hall I found a postcard from Wendy that had slipped under the rug. For a minute I thought it was a message from my mother. The picture showed a dreamy sunset over a platinum blonde beach. I turned it over and read the lyrics that Wendy had copied from "See You in September."

When Aunt Ruby called to say she wouldn't be stopping by that night, I almost broke down on the phone. After the call I listened to the radio for hours, pacing the living room rug, shouting out lyrics to songs I'd learned by heart. I turned on the news and watched for clues to my mother's disappearance. My father would find her tomorrow. Surely he would. She'd come bursting out of her hiding place the minute she heard his voice, unfolding herself from her makeup case, perhaps, wearing too much lipstick and smelling of something flowery.

*

Dad asked how Mom was doing the minute he walked through the front door. When I told him she was missing, that I'd gone too far and made her more afraid of me than she was of the sky falling, his face reddened. I could tell from the way his fingers were pinching the fabric of his summer pants that he wanted to hit me.

He ran around the house crying out "Flo!" Then we heard the faraway sound of her whimper. It wasn't coming from the house, but from somewhere outside. Where?

I hadn't thought to check the crawl space beneath the back porch, that dark cave filled with dead leaves, rusty garden tools and spiders. It was the kind of place I was afraid of. What stunned me now was not that my mother had spent two nights there beneath a ceiling so low she wouldn't even have been able to sit up, but that her terror of me outdid her fear of dirt and darkness and bugs.

Dad crawled in after her. He half dragged, half carried her out. Her face was pale and dirty, her hair matted with leaves and twigs, her nightgown torn and stained. Both her eyes were swollen. She was limp in my father's arms until she saw me standing on the top step of the porch. Then she started kicking and screaming. It sounded like she was hissing at me. Dad held on and squeezed her through the back door past Lissy, who was hopping all over the place and squealing. Mom slipped out of his arms in the middle of the kitchen and fell flat out on the floor, as she'd done on the back porch a few days earlier, clawing at the tiles. My father left her there.

There was too much movement and noise. It was the kind of chaos you see in war films when both sides are shooting and blowing each other up and you can't tell the difference between friend and enemy. I sank down on my haunches, a few feet from Mom. Lissy tried to sit on my lap, but I knocked her off. I kept saying *sorry*. Sorry, sorry, snot running into my mouth.

Dad stepped over me, his heel grazing my forehead, to bend down and whisper something in Mom's ear. The phone seemed to be ringing endlessly. I squeezed my eyes shut, forcing my eyeballs back into my head where I hoped they'd explode.

A familiar voice broke through the chaos.

"Her again?"

"No, my wife this time."

The big-nosed cop, the old guy, stepped over me as one would step over a puddle. He and the young cop plucked my mother up off the floor with no struggle at all. No one said where they were taking her. One of the cops told me to take good care of my sister. He said Mrs. Burr was in the living room and would stay until one of my aunts arrived. I stayed on the kitchen floor for a long time with my back against the stove.

Mrs. Burr had her hands full with Lissy who was hitting herself on the head and uttering horrible little screeches every ten seconds or so. I tried the same thing, slapping myself so hard that something deep inside my brain started throbbing and wouldn't stop.

"I did awful things to my mother," I said to Mrs. Burr, hoping she might forgive me, remind me that I was a kid and didn't have a clue how to stop the sky from falling, but all she did was hand me a stuffed animal from the pile that she'd collected in her attempts to calm Lissy down.

Aunt Veronica showed up about an hour later. I was hoping for Aunt Ruby, who I thought might better understand how a dream son could turn into a nightmare, but apparently she'd gone to be with my parents.

"All we can do is wait," Aunt Veronica said. "Maybe make some brownies, how does that sound?"

"I almost killed my mother," I said. I couldn't help myself. I didn't have the strength to hide one more horror or tell one more lie.

"Oh, don't even think such a thing," Aunt Veronica said. She looked like she was going to hug me but had second thoughts. "You should never have been left alone with her in the first place."

"I forced her to go outside. I tied her arms behind her back," I continued, hoping she would gasp or maybe even slap me across the face.

"What else could you do," she said in the most genuine voice I'd ever heard from her. "I'm sorry to have to be so blunt, but she's completely insane and should have been hospitalized months ago."

I didn't know what to say to that. Was it normal to shove a crazy woman's face into a screen door? Was I honestly trying to help her or was I punishing her for her part in destroying the family?

We had brownies and French fries for supper. Lissy had a brief chocolate high, but then crashed and was in bed by nine o'clock. Aunt Veronica insisted that she and I play Go Fish to take our minds off what had happened today. I let her win because she seemed to need it more than I did. She was so pleased with herself that she let me stay up until past eleven.

I didn't know what to expect of tomorrow: who'd be there, who might have disappeared. For all I knew, both my parents might have been admitted to the mental hospital.

*

I got out of bed the next morning to find Dad in the midst of a fight with Aunt Veronica. His cheeks looked swollen and his hair was a mess.

"It was just a suggestion," she said. "Robby and Melissa need a healthy mother, no matter what it takes."

"What the hell were you thinking?" he asked me, cutting her off. He shoved me against the living room doorframe. "Putting your mother in a jail cell."

"A jail cell?"

"You used to play jail under the porch when you were six. You'd lock poor Louie Burr away for hours at a time."

"I didn't lock Mom anywhere," I said. "I thought I was helping her. Like Dr. McCurl."

"Dr. McCurl is an asshole." He puckered his lips as if he were going to spit. "But she's his now, locked up in the loony bin."

He took a big gulp of air.

"I'm finished fighting. A simple yes or no is all I want, Veronica. Will you stay and look after Lissy today or are your fancy nails more important?"

She stayed and my father padded off to the bathroom. Ten minutes later he was gone. Aunt Veronica tried to pamper me a little, offering me French toast, a little hair trim, but I shook my head at everything she said until she gave up on me and persuaded Lissy to let her braid her hair.

I tried slapping myself on the head again, but the hurt didn't feel good this morning.

★

Days went by in a blur. Aunt Veronica watched Lissy while my father spent all his time either at the Texaco or the hospital. I didn't ask anybody anything and nobody seemed to find that strange. When I picked up the phone one afternoon, Wendy Fergie's voice surprised me. She sounded thin as a stamp. She said her suitcase wasn't unpacked yet, but she could hardly wait to see me. I agreed to meet her at Valhalla Park in an hour though I felt like the dark cloud you never see on a postcard, the bad day no one ever takes a picture of.

On the bike ride down to the Bluffs, I tried to but couldn't remember what Wendy looked like. Even her hands, which I'd held in my own hands, even they escaped me. Large or small? Smooth or rough? I looked at my own fingers on the handlebars and didn't recognize them either. Nothing was the way it had been back in June.

I was different inside and out. I could tell by the way the cuffs of my jeans didn't quite meet my heels that I was taller than I'd been the last day of grade eight. As Aunt Veronica had pointed out, my hair was long. It hung down over my eyes and curled past my collar. I was ready to shave if I could be trusted with a razor blade. It felt like my teeth were bigger too, like a werewolf's. I was hardly the same person who had stood on the edge of the Bluffs beside Wendy making my small effort to tell the truth. I was a monster, someone whose own mother was terrified of him.

Wendy looked like such a little kid. Her hair was short but she had plastic alligator barrettes on both sides of her head. Her blouse was printed with smiling dolphins. After saying hello we were both silent.

"Have a good summer?" she finally asked.

"Lots of changes." I narrowed my eyes like Lonny used to when cigarette smoke drifted into them.

"How's your family?"

"Not so good," I said, wondering whether she'd believe any of what had happened in the last week alone. "What about you?"

"I got tired of being a tourist after a while."

"Yeah?" I couldn't look at her. How hard could it be to be out in the world, discovering new places every day, pampered by loving parents?

"I took lots of pictures. I wished you were there. I'll let you know when I get them developed."

I felt as if something hard and blunt were pushing out of me. I wanted to reach out and mess her hair, untuck her blouse, fumble around for one of her nipples. "It's been a rough summer," I said.

"A long one," she agreed.

I said I had to get going, with no mention of looking for one another when high school started in a few weeks. I left her there in Valhalla Park, her small body outlined against the wide sky. On the ride home, I imagined her pictures: sand castles and starfish, everything gold and pink. A shot of her swell father sticking one of his toes into the surf, another of her mother staring into the sun while lounging on a brightly-coloured towel. Of Wendy herself, standing on the beach, a seashell singing in her ear.

Dad was at the Texaco, Aunt Veronica was talking on the telephone and I was lost in the Classic Comics version of *Crime and Punishment*, imagining myself in every role. The doorbell rang. It was the same two cops who'd investigated everything that happened at our house. The old guy came to the door. The young one was sitting in the cruiser with Lissy.

"What happened? What's wrong?" Aunt Veronica pushed past us onto the front porch.

"We found the young lady up on Kingston Road," he explained. "She almost got into a carful of teenaged boys. In my opinion, she was one step away from…"

Aunt Veronica went kind of limp and leaned against the porch railing.

"I don't know how she got away," she explained. "Can't I even talk on the phone?"

The old guy asked if my father was home, then informed Aunt Veronica that he was handing Lissy over to the Children's Aid.

"I can't risk another incident," he said.

Aunt Veronica tried to argue, but there wasn't really much to say with the word *molested* in the air. She made a quick call to Uncle Maurice who apparently advised her to let the police do their job, that the Children's Aid would be a temporary solution.

While Aunt Veronica packed Lissy's suitcase, I walked out to the cruiser. Lissy was in the back seat and the old cop refused to lower the window. He said I'd have to say goodbye through the glass. I pressed one of my hands to the window and Lissy matched it with one of hers. She didn't seem afraid or upset in any way. Maybe she was enjoying having one adventure after another.

Once she was gone, Aunt Veronica called Dad at the Texaco. "Ed, the police have taken Melissa away. I packed her pink rabbit and her Sunday shoes…"

That was all she got out before Dad started yelling. I could hear him raging from across the room. She held the phone away from her ear and finally thrust it at me.

"Stop it," was the only thing I could think to say. The yelling stopped.

"What the hell is going on?" he asked.

"The Children's Aid," I said, picturing a hospital ward with dozens of warm, friendly nurses. A terrible silence ensued, then a long sigh. He didn't have a single yell left in him.

"Jesus H. Christ," he said. "There's not much left to lose."

NINE

I KNEW THERE WERE PEOPLE who'd have a fit if they heard about my mother being in a mental hospital and my sister in a foster home—like I used to be shocked by the Costellos' drinking, or Lonny Milford and his dying father. My mother is crazy. I said it over and over again. Sometimes it hurt, sometimes it didn't.

My own father lapsed into a silent funk. After days at the Texaco followed by early evening visits with my mother at the Queen Street Mental Hospital, he would shuffle home, dropping all that held his body together onto the couch. After a couple of nights, I got up the nerve to ask him about the hospital.

"What it's like there?" I made sure not to ask about Mom directly. I kept picturing her in a padded cell and begging not to have to see me ever again.

"A real palace," he said, snorting. "It's a loony bin. What did you expect, the Royal York?"

"Is there any other place that might be nicer?"

"She's had a complete breakdown," he said, watching to see what the word did to me. "There's no such thing as nice for her."

He fluttered through a *Popular Mechanics* and tried to swallow the frog in his throat. He turned off the reading lamp and sat in the semi-dark, his arms wrapped around a blue hippopotamus, one of

Lissy's stuffed animals, his chin buried in the hippo's fuzzy snout.

"I don't have the time or energy for another heart attack," he said. Those blissful days of recovery with the Monopoly games and the singalongs, all of us pretending that nothing was wrong—they were gone.

What if he'd been the one to get agoraphobia? He was too strong to be forced out onto the back porch. Probably he'd have immersed himself in the fear until he grew tired of being cooped up. "So what if the sky falls," he'd have said, and then moved on.

★

A social worker named Miss Clairy arranged for us to talk to Lissy on the phone the next evening.

"Don't they realize she's retarded?" Dad stood as far away from the phone as possible without leaving the room. It was my job to answer by the second ring. I listened to Miss Clairy as she described how wonderfully Lissy was doing.

"She's just come in from playing badminton and is drinking lemonade," she reported, like Lissy was some kind of athlete. "Here she is now. Say hello, Lissy." Silence.

"Lissy, it's Robby. How are you doing?"

I heard a recognizable Lissy laugh followed by a thump and a clatter. In the background a radio was playing a song by The Supremes. Someone was clapping their hands off the beat.

"Lissy, it's me. Want to say hi to Queen Mary? Want to talk to Dad?"

A squeak, a giggle, then finally a sort of word, "Fweet," repeated twice.

"There." Miss Clairy was back on the phone, already recapping what to her had been a landmark chat. "She's gone out to tell the other children about her special telephone call."

"All she said was 'Fweet.' I don't know what that means."

"Oh, it's probably something she loves and wanted to share with you. Maybe 'sweet,' like her lemonade. We'll arrange a visit

144

soon and you can ask her yourself."

Trying to think like Perry Mason, I remembered that Lissy's mangled words didn't follow particular rules, that her mistakes were always different. Letters might be added anywhere, sometimes two or three in one measly word. Fweet, for example: what if the W should have been an R and the T didn't belong there at all.

"I'm free, I'm free," was what I decided she'd said.

★

Aunt Ruby dropped by to pick up some of Mom's clothes. It was the first time I'd seen her since the day I'd driven Mom to take refuge in the crawl space. I was sure she'd be furious with me, refuse to look me in the eye, maybe even call me names. But she walked straight up to me when she entered the house and hugged me hard and long.

I didn't realize how many tears were stored behind my eyes until I started crying. I soaked Aunt Ruby's shoulder.

"I didn't mean to hurt her," I sobbed. I was gulping a sort of hiccup between the words.

"Oh, Robby," she sighed, "you should never have had to handle such a huge responsibility. You're so mature that everyone forgets you're just fourteen years old."

Deep breaths of her vanilla-scented perfume were helping me calm down enough to control the hiccupping.

"But the things I did…"

"Hush," she said. "You were trying to do the impossible, and that's that."

I remembered Mom telling Dr. McCurl how she'd been babied her whole life, never allowed to strike out on her own, or face consequences, or figure out ways to cope with a crazy world. Aunt Ruby might call me mature, but I was still a child in her version of what had happened. Whatever I'd done was someone else's fault.

I tried again to take some responsibility. "I tied her hands," I said.

"You didn't know what else to do," she responded, pulling me back into a hug that this time felt like a headlock.

*

Grammie Gorman landed on our doorstep looking years younger and determined to take control.

"You took a cab from the airport?" Dad asked, more shocked by the thought of Grammie braving Toronto streets than of her flying across the Atlantic.

"I've travelled in worse things than taxicabs," she snapped. She dumped her scuffed suitcases in the front hallway. "What's this I hear about Florence? Locked up under the back porch?"

Dad, who had practically stopped talking to everyone else, stumbled his way through an abridged version of the story and finished up with "Robby pushed her over the edge trying to play doctor."

"He pushed her off the back porch?" Grammie looked ready to slug me.

Dad glared at me as if this was now his story. "He upset her so much that she got under the porch on her own."

Grammie glanced at me, then back at my father. "Isn't that a good thing?" she asked. "At least it got her out of the house."

"That's certainly one way of looking at it," Dad said, letting loose a sigh like air rushing out of a balloon.

"Well, at least you've managed to hold on to the cat," Grammie said. She pointed at Queen Mary, grooming her tail on the living room rug. Then she nodded at me. "I'm surprised you haven't found somewhere else for Robinson to live."

Dad and I looked at one another, entertaining the possibility.

"I might as well lend a hand," Grammie said. "I'll stay until Florence walks back in through the front door."

Dad pulled his Texaco cap out of his rear pocket and slapped it down on his head.

"Gotta close up the station," he said, brushing past her.

146

How could Grammie call what she was offering us help? The only two people in this family who'd ever needed her were my mother and Lissy, and she'd run out on both of them. She'd as much as told me I was in charge.

She seemed dazzled by all the afternoon light, not having seen the curtains open since midwinter.

"Isn't anyone going to ask me about Europe?" she asked.

"Who's anyone?" I said. "There's just you and me."

She looked at me queerly, as if I'd spoken Russian or told her she had an ugly big toe.

"Where do I begin?" she asked, letting me get away with the sarcasm. "The Louvre? The Coliseum? The Parthenon?" She stepped back into the hall and unzipped a suitcase, pulling out reams of brochures. She brought them into the living room and dumped them on the coffee table.

"Feel free to peruse."

All the colourful destinations of the world: Wendy Fergie and her photos, Grammie and her brochures. Maybe I should have been collecting pictures of my summer: crawl space, mental hospital, foster home.

*

My first day at Scarborough Bluffs Secondary School was an ordeal. There were so many textbooks in my knapsack, I felt like the Hunchback of Notre Dame. Jockstraps, prefects and detention class. School colours: *Go gold and blue!* I was homesick for the single classroom and my old desk. I missed independent studies, Mrs. Gandhi and LBJ, all my fantasies of saving the world. I never once caught sight of Marco, Louie or Dana in the crowded halls. I had a sinking feeling that I'd get lost and never find the physics lab or the gymnasium.

Before we were allowed to go home, the entire student body met in the auditorium for a pep talk from the principal, a ruddy-faced man named Mr. Haam. I sat by myself in the last row. Whenever

Mr. Haam called for school spirit, a forest of fists appeared in the air. When he ordered a cheer, a chorus of cheers rose up. I sat there, waiting for it all to be over, then was almost crushed in the rush of one thousand stirred-up students racing out into the Scarborough streets.

On my second day, Wendy suddenly appeared in the hustle of the cafeteria, wearing a bright red-and-yellow paisley dress with a matching hair band.

"I've got the picture" is what I thought she said, meaning she'd figured out how to fit in. But when she spread a summer's worth of sunny, fun-filled Maritime snapshots all over the table, I realized she'd been as lost as I was.

"I promised I'd show you these," she said.

In each and every one of them, Wendy was pleading for me to look at her, waving from hills, leaping out of waves, scaling rocks, eating, daydreaming, walking, fishing, frowning, her hair windblown, her eyes round and wide. It was all too much for me. I was no longer smart and resourceful, sitting up on that billboard ledge on Danforth Avenue, dangling my feet above a doll-like world. The afternoons we'd spent together in Valhalla Park seemed years ago, kid stuff. How could someone as normal as Wendy even begin to understand what had happened to me over the summer? I closed my eyes, shutting out Wendy and her sickening innocence. The cafeteria roared around me. The shuffling sound close at hand was Wendy collecting her photographs, putting them back in the envelope. When I opened my eyes, she was gone.

*

Grammie started cornering Dad the minute he walked through the door.

"So, how is she?"

She would have preferred to get her information first-hand, but Mom had refused to see anyone other than Dad.

"How's Florence, Ed?"

"The same," he'd say, scratching the back of his hand or rubbing his elbow.

"Poor creature," Grammie would reply.

What would she say to me if she knew how hard I'd pushed the poor creature? Not even Dad knew the whole story. At first I was afraid that once she felt safe at the hospital, Mom would accuse me of trying to kill her. But the worst of it seemed to be our secret, which made me feel all the more alone.

While Grammie was watching the *Merv Griffin Show* in the rec room one day after school, I examined the route between my parent's bedroom and the front door. No signs of how Mom had dragged her heels on the living room carpet or where she had clawed at the doorframe. I pressed my face into the screen so the wire mesh stung my flesh and drew back, surprised. I was trying to relive our last walk along the hall, but I couldn't bring back what I wanted: that short-lived, powerful feeling of accomplishment.

★

Equipped with jockstraps and all decked out in white t-shirts and shorts for the first PE class, some of us were hauling ourselves up twenty-foot ropes while Coach Dickens led the rest through claps and jeers.

"Climb that sucker, you meatball," Coach hollered, his cheeks the same carrot-orange as his brush cut and moustache. "Wrap your balls around it, fairy face."

Whenever a climber would pause mid-climb, he'd snap the end of the rope and send him sailing through the air like Tarzan on a vine. One of the fatter boys fell six feet, missing the safety mat entirely and twisting his ankle on the hard gym floor.

"Powder puff! Crybaby!" Coach hurled insults like a tennis ball machine gone crazy. He got everyone so worked up that they began inventing their own nicknames: *Faggot Breath. Jerk-Off Brain. Pussy Machine.* I watched Alex Mitchell, the class clown, burn a strip on his palms the colour of raw hamburger. Joey Blake, the class geek, went into hysterics at eight feet. When Tony Salvarinas, the class beast, made it up, he banged on the gymnasium rafters, screaming, "I'm the king of the whole friggin' school."

"Candy ass! Eunuch!"

Long before it was my turn, I decided I would not climb. I was a Tedley, best measured by my refusals. If I agreed to scramble up into the gymnasium's rafters for no good reason other than obedience, there was no telling what I'd do next.

"Okay, Tedley, move your ass!"

"No." I held myself perfectly still and straight.

"What did you say?"

"I said no."

Coach froze for a moment, staring at me like there had to be a punchline. He strode across the safety mat to where I was standing.

"Sissy?" he asked, slow and loud. "Scaredy-cat?"

It wasn't a question of bravery; I wasn't terrified of heights. I didn't have a problem with strength either. Twenty feet wouldn't have totalled me. But there was no way I was going to scramble up a rope because some prick of a gym teacher ordered me to. I wondered if Lonny Milford had ever climbed the ropes in this very gymnasium. It seemed like the sort of senseless thing he might have done for the hell of it.

Coach's hands flew out of his pockets. He grabbed the rope and flung it at me. The thick knot hit me on the side of my head and knocked me clear off my feet.

"Pantywaist! Chicken Boy!"

As soon as I could focus, I got up and walked away from the mat and out to the locker room. A part of me was crushed, but there was a deeper part that felt free.

★

Saturday morning Miss Clairy picked us up in her station wagon and drove us to the west end to make our first visit to Lissy's temporary new home. It turned out to be really cool, with a big, open backyard that stretched all the way out into a meadow. Mr. and Mrs. Kish, the foster parents, a chubby, happy-go-lucky couple, stayed in the background, letting Miss Clairy gush on about how wonderful it all was, as if she were selling us real estate.

"The property is two acres." She waved her hands around as she talked, making everything seem bigger than it actually was. "There's the swing," she said, pointing between two oak trees. "And over there is a little garden where Melissa has her own row of marigolds. And, of course, in that marvellous empty field, the children can gallop like horses."

"My granddaughter is a child, not a horse," Grammie said stiffly.

Miss Clairy blushed. "I'm only trying to tell you how happy Melissa is here."

I could feel Dad bristling beside me, but before Miss Clairy could provoke him into exploding, a herd of her horses came bounding around the side of the house, Lissy, tall and thrilling, in the lead.

"Here they are now," Miss Clairy announced.

Six pairs of thundering feet, six children ranging in age from maybe nine to Lissy's seventeen. Three boys, three girls. All like Lissy. She grabbed my hands and spun us in a wide circle, pretty much ignoring Dad but howling at the sight of Grammie. She nestled against her in a brief hug then led her five friends over to the swing.

"Well, she certainly seems lively enough," said Grammie, "although I'd feel better if she were calmer. Is all this running around healthy?" Without waiting for an answer, she shouted, "Melissa, come over here so I can get a good look at you."

Lissy stopped and stared. She made a few clucking sounds, pressing her tongue against the roof of her mouth, and took off for the empty field, her friends close behind. Miss Clairy gracefully blocked Grammie's way.

"Let her be," she said. "She's just exercising her independence, like any normal adolescent."

Dad was the first to turn back to the car, followed by Miss Clairy. When Lissy was doll-sized in the distance, I turned away, leaving Grammie standing there to watch alone.

★

When I spotted our black Valiant parked outside the main doors by the flagpole after school, I thought I must be seeing things. Or was I about to be shipped off to some foster home too? Then another thought crossed my mind—Mom had died and Dad was going to drive me to the cemetery so I could dig her narrow grave in an act of penance. I was ready for anything as I slipped into the passenger seat.

"What's up?" I asked, trying hard to sound like I didn't care.

"Nothing much. I thought we might take a drive, have a chat."

Maybe Coach Dickens had called to complain about my refusal to climb that bloody rope. Maybe I was being kicked out of school.

"Okay," I said, my head reeling with possibilities, everything from Dr. McCurl wanting to meet with me in order to formally blame me for what I did to my mother, to the police deciding to charge me with attempted murder.

We drove up to Kingston Road, into the nitty-gritty of Scarborough, its endless plazas, its dirty white apartment buildings and seedy motels. Stoplight after stoplight, we drove on, mostly in silence, Dad occasionally reading a billboard out loud or pointing at an unleashed dog. When we'd passed a huge, junky used car lot, he veered unexpectedly onto a side street and parked in front of a lopsided green and white house.

"Who lives here?" I asked.

He shrugged his shoulders as if he didn't know or care. He shifted his knees out from under the steering wheel so he could face me.

"You know what I heard today?"

I shook my head slowly. Big black moths were flying around

in there.

"The South African Prime Minister was stabbed to death in the Capetown Parliament, right in front of the entire government, in broad daylight. Here one minute, gone the next."

"That's awful."

"Every minute wasted is a minute lost," he continued, dead serious. "You think you have time to be miserable, then bang, you don't have any time. No time left at all."

The word *bang* didn't fit with the South African stabbing, but nothing my father was saying quite fit together. I simply nodded whenever I thought he expected a response.

"I've been trying to carry on normally for your sake, Robby. But losing both my wife and my daughter has left a hole in me. I can't keep pretending that life goes on and on like this. You understand how messed up everything is."

He paused to take a huge dry swallow.

"My heart feels like it's being stabbed on a daily basis."

What could I say to that? For a second, I thought about jumping out of the car, running up to the green and white house, pounding on the door and pleading with them to let me in. But Dad kept on explaining.

"You're still a kid, Robby. Your whole life is ahead of you, but all I've got is the here and now."

He looked absolutely miserable. It would have been easier if he'd started to cry or accused me of somehow having used up all his time.

"What do you want to do?" I asked finally, surprised by the strength of my own voice.

"I'd like to go up to Grey Bay for a few days. I think I'm ready to start building that cabin."

I waited for more, but Grey Bay turned out to be the only thing.

"So, go," I said, turning away and staring out the front window.

"You don't mind if I don't stay home with you and Grammie?" His side of the car seemed to grow lighter. Part of him was already gone.

"Do what you like." I had to stop myself from punching the dashboard. It helped to shrug, so I did, three times.

"Maybe you could even visit your Mom at the hospital. I think it's about time you saw her."

He patted me on the knee, started up the car and pulled away from the green and white house where apparently someone even less important than me lived.

★

Instead of listening to the teacher drone on about China, I doodled a map of my life on the fly-leaf of my geography textbook. The mental hospital was a big question mark in the middle. Further down the page I made a sloppy circle for Grey Bay. For Lissy at Mr. and Mrs. Kish's foster home, I chose a star. I scattered everyone else all over the place. Grammie's Europe was a series of cloud-like swirls at the top left-hand corner. Roma had started private school that fall, so she was a tiny dollar sign. Lonny Milford was empty white space beside a skull and bones depicting Mr. Milford's grave. I used checkmarks for my three friends: Marco, who had joined the Scarborough Bluffs football team and didn't have much time for me anymore; Dana, who'd been drawn into the Drama Club and was already rehearsing to play Tiny Tim in the December production of *A Christmas Carol*; and Louie, who was registered in the four-year Business and Technology course, way over on the other side of the school. A heart with an X across it for Wendy Fergie, who was far away in 9B. Tits for the Remington twins in that other country called grade ten. The page filled up. For myself, I drew a hanged man in the bottom left-hand corner of the page, his neck already broken.

I didn't seem to have room in my head for schoolwork. Keeping track of where everyone had gone crowded my mind. I had to be very careful not to do anything that might cause more trouble or confusion. I didn't know the answers to teachers' questions. When was the War of the Roses? What are the three major classes of rocks? What colour does starch turn in the presence of iodine? What does X equal if Y equals 9? How many lines in a sonnet? I kept my eyes down and hoped I wouldn't be called on. I used to be smart, now I was simply muddled.

My English teacher, Mrs. Keating, was the only one who didn't write me off. She was a big blonde woman whose hair was always falling in her eyes. She wore outfits with so many ties and buttons that it must have taken her ages to get dressed in the morning. She'd been choosing me to read out loud when we play-acted Shakespeare.

The day I played Romeo, Mrs. Keating pushed me to the front of the class, pairing me up with near-sighted, buck-toothed Gabby Tucker. I knelt beside her where she lay on the floor pretending to be dead. Everyone giggled. My ears were burning, my fingers prickling.

"Ah! dear Juliet," I cried. "Why art thou yet so fair?" Gabby Tucker had her eyes open, watching me carefully, but I blinked at her slowly a couple of times until she got the hint. What must Romeo have felt, staring at the only person in the world who truly loved him?

"Eyes, look your last!" I slapped Juliet lightly on both cheeks, something I'd seen on an old episode of *Ben Casey*.

"Arms, take your last embrace!" I wrenched Juliet into my arms and dragged her up onto my knees.

I could hear the class getting restless, which made the blood rush powerfully into my ears. I had to hurry up and drink the poison.

"Here's to my love!" I gulped a fistful of air. "O true apothecary! Thy drugs are quick. Thus with a kiss I die."

God, it felt good to die. I collapsed on top of Gabby, both of us deflating.

Gabby was crying softly beneath me, but I thought she might still be in character. Mrs. Keating grabbed me by the shoulders. None of the other kids were giggling now. Everyone looked a little afraid.

I would have considered it a blessing had the sky chosen that moment to come crashing down on the entire school. I took a deep breath and apologized to both Mrs. Keating and Gabby, who by this time was back on her feet, her spine pressed against the blackboard. I returned to my desk without looking at any of my classmates.

I was in a daze for the rest of the week. The classrooms were hot, the teachers' voices muffled. The squeal of chalk on the blackboard gave me shivers. I was nauseous before the first bell rang in the morning. Kids passing me in the halls kept nudging one another.

"That's the kid who Romeo-ed Gabby Tucker!"

The kid who wouldn't climb the ropes, the kid who Coach Dickens almost knocked cold, the kid who never brought his brains to class. Once upon a time, back at the Kingston Road Public School, Miss Luther had called me gifted. But after less than a month at high school, I was famous for being a disobedient, anarchistic, raging psycho. I stared hard at the floors as I walked the halls, wishing to drown in my own dim shadow. Several times I almost slammed into a wall, once I almost fell down a flight of stairs. I was finally going crazy.

One day I heard music coming from an open locker, a mauve transistor radio dangling from the top shelf by its plastic strap. Wendy's locker. Wendy's radio. Wendy's song. I was so glad to see her, I forgot all about our rift.

"Wendy," I said, taking a step toward her.

She shrunk back into the open locker as if it were an escape hatch. I could almost hear the clang of the slammed door and Wendy's tinny voice screaming for help.

"It's okay," I said. "I'm not going to hurt you."

The wariness broadcast all over her face didn't change much once I'd spoken, but her feet appeared more solidly planted on the floor.

"Things have gotten so messed up," I said. "I wish I could run away to the Maritimes," I continued, hoping this might please her a bit.

"I hated being in the Maritimes without you," she said. "I couldn't wait to get back home, but then you…"

"You wouldn't say that if you knew what happened, what I did to my mother."

A big, glossy tear appeared in the corner of Wendy's right eye and hung there. Her left eye was swimming in what could easily turn into a stream of tears. She lifted a hand from her side, but instead of wiping away the tear, reached out and ran her fingers down my cheek.

"How do you know what I'll say?" she asked. "Give me a chance."

The big tear fell, and another. I made a gesture to wipe away the wet, but Wendy flinched and took another step back.

"You might as well have dropped my heart off the Scarborough Bluffs," she said. "You wouldn't even look at my pictures."

"Pictures of you having a perfect summer."

"Pictures of me missing you," she corrected, turning away to pull a pink sweater from the hook inside her locker. She shut the door and snapped the lock shut.

"Can I walk you home?" I asked.

"I thought you wanted to run away," she said.

Did I? I couldn't think straight. Was this what Romeo had done: given up too easily? "Help," I said, so quietly that not even the locker could have heard, but Wendy was already out of sight.

★

A foolproof way to convince Grammie that I was too ill to go to school was to lie on my back as if paralyzed and moan softly. When she asked me what was the matter, I whimpered a little, moving nothing but my lips. Grammie poked and prodded until she was satisfied that I was hopeless. The truth was, I didn't feel very well. By noon my back ached from lying in bed. I bundled myself up in my flannel dressing gown, wandered into the living room and collapsed into the easy chair by the front window.

I stared out at the street for a while, trying to forget things. Then a big moving van pulled up in front of the Milfords'. Two burly guys lumbered into the house, reappearing a few minutes later with a blue couch on their shoulders. Over the next hour, they hauled away hassocks and rugs, mattresses and cardboard boxes. A dining room table sailed through the air like a ghost ship. A bookshelf appeared, naked without books. They dragged out a large wooden trunk, bumping it down the porch steps. Each jolt gave me a weird feeling, as if my heart were slammed through a basketball hoop. I was sure Lonny was inside, hunched on his knees, his spine curled into a hump, ass in the air, the end of an orphan's story, no matter how tough he'd acted. Tossed out with the ashtrays and laundry baskets, the frying pans and electric drills.

Most likely Lonny had played Romeo to a few girls in his day. What a fucking laugh, thinking I had something in common with Lonny Milford. But the truth was we both knew what it felt like to be so angry that we were willing to hurt someone, to do stupid things, to rail against the world until the world gave up and left us alone. I had no idea what had happened to Lonny's mother, but she was gone. He must have been powerless to stop her, and twice as powerless when he had to let his father die. I realized that I missed Lonny and wished I'd had the sense to tell him, when I'd had the chance, what had been going on inside me. He might have been able to help me cope with the fear and the rage. At the very least, we could have screamed together, shaking our fists at the clouds.

*

Grammie gave me one more day to languish. I probably hadn't fooled her; a woman like Grammie has seen it all. She felt sorry for me, I guess.

How comforting it often had been in grade eight to lose myself in India or Vietnam. So on my first day back to school, I read the assigned chapter for History at lunch hour, and when I was asked in class to give the goods on Henry the Eighth, I repeated what I'd read, transforming myself into the text. Same with Physics the next day, then Geography. People were still whispering around me, but their suspicions lifted a little.

When I arrived home on Friday afternoon, Grammie was waiting at the front door, gloves and purse ready for an outing.

"We're going to visit your mother," she announced, taking my elbow and steering me back to the street.

We boarded a bus on Kingston Road that took us down to Queen Street, where we switched to a streetcar. I tried to focus on everything I saw—stores and restaurants, trucks and baby carriages—but the traffic and the noise rattled me and brought on the nausea again. It felt like riding an electric chair.

The Queen Street Mental Hospital, or 999 as it was commonly called for its street number, was every bit as eerie as I'd imagined. High stone walls, bars on some of the upper windows. It was the kind of place the ghosts of witches and wolves might be banished to after being booted out of fairy tales.

Grammie led me down long, cold halls, a maze of twists and turns. I heard coughs from behind closed doors. I heard a high-pitched wail. There were lots of unsettling smells: stale tobacco, roast beef and bleach. At my mother's ward, a nurse directed us into a light-filled room. I expected something like a coal mine, dark and damp, but this room was full of windows. Several women were lounging on couches, basking in the sun as if they were at the beach. Some wore blue robes and pajamas, some wore ordinary street clothes, and a couple of women were smoking long, slim cigarettes. None of them resembled my mother, so it shocked me when Grammie yoo-hooed at a woman who was facing in the other direction. Mom turned to us, smiled and waved. I'd pictured her in a straitjacket, lying on the floor of a closet-size padded cell, her eyes wild, the palms of her hands dirty. I'd never dreamt that she'd be neat and trim, her hair dyed blonde again, her fingernails painted pink. I'd never imagined her in a room full of windows.

How Grammie was able to chat was beyond me, but she was famous for always having something to say. I sat there in a pool of light and stared. Mom didn't look afraid, or worried, or furious, just a tiny bit dazed, her words coming slower than usual, like she was sucking on a piece of toffee. Chat, laugh, relax, she could do it all. She looked at me every now and again, but seemed puzzled. Once she reached out and dabbed at the corner of my mouth. I wondered if she was trying to get me to smile.

There was no mention of those two days beneath the back porch, or the awful things I had done to make her seek such a horrifying refuge. I closed my eyes for a moment and pictured her wearing that filthy white nightgown, kicking and screaming in my father's arms when she caught sight of me.

"So," Grammie said loudly, as if about to give a speech to the entire sun porch, "any idea when you'll be coming home?"

"Dr. McCurl says I have a way to go yet."

"Well, you're obviously not afraid of windows anymore." Grammie nodded at all the light.

"Windows were never the problem. There's a great big world out there that I have to get used to all over again."

I wished I were six and could sit in her lap and let her fingers comb the light into my hair. When Grammie and I stood up to leave, she leaned forward to kiss me goodbye. I received the kiss standing dumb as a chair, as dumb as I had sat throughout the visit. You'd have thought I was the patient.

*

Once Grammie had gone to bed that night, her snores deep and uniform, I snuck out onto the back porch. The smell of rain-to-come was in the air. The entire yard was one moving shadow play, the sky above a streaky charcoal grey, three-quarters of the moon smothered under what looked like a dark blanket. What a perfect night for a meteor to plummet into our yard.

The handle of the crawl space door shone pale silver like the pin on a grenade. I was half-convinced it would burn me when I reached out to touch it. I had to know what it felt like to crawl on hands and knees across the cold earth floor, to turn around halfway in and crawl back again to close the door, cutting off the only light other than what fell through cracks between the boards, what it was like to lie in darkness, hour after hour, over forty-eight hours in total, terrified of every noise, of every uncontrollable thought.

I crouched down and fumbled with the handle. As the door swung outwards, I could feel the drop in temperature. I inched forward, creeping into this cave of spiders and centipedes. It smelled like rot, with a whiff of something yeasty, like a loaf of Wonder Bread just opened. Once I could turn and lie back on my elbows, it was actually kind of cozy. Maybe Mom appreciated having the ceiling only inches from her face. The tightness of the space, coupled with the dark, made it seem like the kind of place where something transformative might happen.

But my awareness narrowed in on the sensations in my body, the world of knees, hips and shoulder blades. There was both too little of me and too much. Whatever thought crossed my mind, I became it. *Cold*, I thought, and felt the pinch of cold. *Terrified*, I thought, as the hairs on the back of my neck stood up. I was closed up inside Mr. Milford's coffin. I was the golf ball that rolled under Lonny's car. I was my mother after I'd tied her hands behind her back.

Panic was squeezing my lungs. I had to get out of there. I started to scramble back, bumping my head and cutting my baby finger on what might have been a rock or a tooth. I finally threw myself against the door and burst out, collapsing on the dark lawn below the vast night sky. The slow wheel of the stars was something to lie beneath, something beautiful.

My mother tried to be as small as an apron pocket, a tiny fold of curtain, a last note squeezed from her accordion, but she had called out for help before she completely disappeared.

TEN

I WALKED INTO GYM CLASS the first day of October, ready for absolutely anything. As far as I was concerned, Coach Dickens was a tyrant, but I felt more positive toward the boys in the class after my visit to 999, where it had been hard to tell the difference between patients and visitors. My first big step as an ordinary Scarborough Bluffs Secondary School student was to lead the lineup at Dickens' current torture device, the trampoline. Grammie would have been proud. I waited until the other kids were jostling one another in an effort not to have to go first, then took my place.

Up on the trampoline I lost my balance immediately. *I am a trampoline,* I said under my breath, getting to my feet. Slowly I began taking tiny jumps, building the jumps bit by bit until I hit my stride, risking tall, rocketing leaps. I hurled myself into thin air, rotating in a somersault. The class was egging me on. Coach Dickens' mouth was wide open. If I could so alter my whole reputation with a mere flip, imagine what I could accomplish with a backward somersault. I leapt higher, throwing my legs over my shoulders. For a second it felt like my neck might snap, but I gave my hips an extra push and away I went, landing on my knees, shaky but still bouncing a little, to cheering and applause.

★

Dad arrived home from Grey Bay late the next afternoon. He walked in trance-like, as if he'd just finished a hard day's work at the Texaco and was longing for his slippers and pipe. He muttered hello to Grammie, who was doing some hand washing in the kitchen sink, and tossed a howdy-do to me. He sank into his easy chair, where Queen Mary parked herself on his lap, the Saturday *Toronto Star* protecting him like the Berlin Wall.

"There are a few things that need fixing around here, Ed," Grammie announced, pulling a neatly folded piece of paper from her apron pocket. She always ignored being ignored.

Dad grunted, his mind already deep into world news. He held the main section up in front of his face, showing a photograph of a Viet Cong prisoner staring at the tip of a bayonet, but nothing could stop Grammie. She poked a finger at the soldier's chest, pushing the paper into Dad's nose.

"The house is going to pot," she said. "I've made a list."

The world is going to pot, I wanted to say. Grammie launched into her list of complaints. Cracked toilet seat, flickering lamp, faulty stove element, leaky basement laundry tub, dead kettle plus a pile of bills.

"I'm sorry," Dad said, "but I don't have the time for all those things. There's the Texaco, there's Flo, and there's my own health."

"You can't fit a toilet seat in there somewhere?"

"The world's full of wrack and ruin," he said, settling the pages of *The Star* around him again.

Grammie tried to keep up the fight. She accused him of laziness, unmanliness. Dad refused to strike back. He turned another page to stay buried in world news. Finally, she surrendered, took a last look at her list, sighed, crumpled it in her fist and dropped it in his lap.

★

I wanted to go back to the beginning of 1966 and start all over again. I wanted to be stronger, saner, less involved. During our next visit with Lissy, I saw how much I needed her home with me. I wanted the two of us watching *The Secret Storm* or sucking on Popsicles or trying to tie Queen Mary's bushy tail into a loop. No matter what anyone else said, Lissy was a major part of my normal life. So while Dad sat there glumly with Miss Clairy, and Grammie investigated the place more thoroughly, her nose twitching like a bloodhound's, I joined up with Lissy and her pack of followers, linking myself to the end of the line in a never-ending game of Follow the Leader. We pounded our feet, swung from branches, hopped, skipped and jumped, whatever Lissy the Leader chose to do.

Gradually I moved up the line. Eventually, right behind Lissy, I grabbed her by the waist and veered off, taking over first position and bringing the whole procession to a halt. Lissy kicked at the lawn a couple of times, mad as hell, but when I started skipping she pushed one of the younger boys aside and skipped behind me. Soon everyone was skipping. We were brother and sister, a real team. No fake family of foster kids could truly take my place. She was crying when I climbed into the back seat of Miss Clairy's car. She even tried to climb through the window after me.

"Sweetie pie, don't you want to stay here with all your friends?" Miss Clairy cooed, but Lissy ignored her, with tears streaming down her cheeks.

"You ought to be ashamed," Grammie snapped. I knew she'd be on the phone next morning, stepping up her struggle to get Lissy back home.

★

Our family visit with Lissy sank Dad further into the dumps. He was so depressed he could hardly lift his knife and fork at dinner that night.

"What are you trying to do, turn the milk sour?" Grammie asked.

Dad glared at her. "It's shaping up to be a hard week at the Texaco. Head office is sending some new efficiency expert to spend a day evaluating our operation. I've got to get up to the Bay either Thursday or Friday to talk to a guy who's going to build me a fieldstone fireplace, plus, I promised Flo I'd pick up some peanut brittle, but I didn't make it to Laura Secord's before they closed, and I've got to make a follow-up appointment with the cardiologist."

"Sounds to me like a simple case of too much to do," Grammie said.

"I'm smart enough to know that if you want a good job done, you'd better do it yourself," he said, mashing his fork into a carrot.

"Mr. All Alone. What a sorry role," Grammie said, fake-sniffling. "When are you going to learn to stop letting Flo wrap you around her finger?"

"Flo's sick."

"Not so sick that she can't enjoy a box of peanut brittle. She's in a lovely sun porch, painting her nails and eating candy. Why should she get well?"

My father's head wobbled a little. He looked like he might scream, cry and stick out his tongue all at the same time. "Well, what do you want me to do?" he asked.

"Drop some of the load. Talk to us at dinnertime. Let Flo know she has no choice but to get well."

"And if she refuses or drifts away from me, leaves me?"

"She won't leave you over a package of peanut brittle." Grammie gave him one of her best velvet-painting looks.

A tear fell from his eye and landed on his fork. Dad had taught me at least half of what I knew about being alone. The possibility of more tears so freaked me out I had to leave the table.

★

I spotted Wendy going into the variety store with a couple of her girlfriends. I waited outside, trying not to look like I was lurking.

"Wendy!" I did my best to sound surprised. "Fancy meeting you here," I said, wincing. I recalled how phony Roma sounded when she was trying to be cool. "Do you think we could talk for a minute?"

"Maybe," she said, looking over my shoulder into the window display: a jack-o'-lantern surrounded by candy kisses and brightly-coloured fallen leaves. She glanced at the friends with raised eyebrows and they moved off.

"I wanted to let you know that my mother is in the hospital now, a mental hospital, but she's slowly getting better." I hurried on. "She's already asking for peanut brittle."

Wendy was listening. I could tell by the steadiness of her gaze.

"My sister's in a temporary foster home and my father went up to his cabin to get away from it all. But my grandmother made it back from Europe in one piece."

A trickle of sweat ran down my spine.

"And I... I..." I stuttered, unsure how to condense myself into one sentence. "I had too much on my plate," I said, taking the words out of my father's mouth. "I went a little crazy there for a while."

Wendy stood her ground, as if I hadn't said nearly enough, but then her eyes began to flicker. "Life can get really hard sometimes," she said.

"You're right."

"It's enough to drive you to drink," she continued. "Anyway, that's what my Dad always says."

Leaves were swirling at our feet, dancing in the wind.

"I've got to get going now," Wendy said. "But thanks for being so real."

I tried to fit a little hope into my goodbye smile. "See you," I said.

"Soon," Wendy added.

★

Marco and I were hanging out. He'd overheard a couple of grade nine girls refer to my Romeo performance as 'cool.'

"And to think, you came this close to being a total geek." he said.

"So how's football practice going?"

"Franny Remington actually talked to me in the hall when I was wearing my uniform. Next thing you know, she'll be giving me a private viewing."

"Are you sure it wasn't Lucy."

"I'll take whatever I can get." Same old Marco under a quarterback's helmet.

"I guess you heard about my Mom being in the hospital."

Marco nodded.

"And Lissy's in a foster home."

"Lucky you're so cool," he said. "Otherwise people might think your family is cursed."

"Fucked is more like it," I said.

Marco laughed and grabbed me around the neck, as if he were tackling, and threw me to the ground.

*

The air was crisp and fresh. The backyard light burned yellow-orange and red. The trees were completely bald, squirrels scurrying across the branches like high wire artists. Queen Mary carefully picked her way through the leaves as if walking through snakes.

Dad usually attacked the lawn, wielding the rake vigorously, but his moves today were slow and easy, floating the leaves into neat piles. He stopped often, leaning lazily on his rake and staring up at the sky.

"It's all attitude," he said.

I knew what he meant, but attitude seemed too fragile a scaffold to hang his hope on. Sure enough, twenty minutes later he was raking madly again, and I could tell by his irritable huffing that he was dying to complain about his lot in life.

On my first visit to 999 alone, the sun porch was crowded with patients and visitors. All the light and noise made me nauseous. But when Mom joined me, I pretended that everything was fine. She looked really good, her hair all springy. She was dressed in slacks and a pink sweater, the kind of outfit ordinary women wore. She grabbed me by the hand and pulled me toward the exit. Other visitors were watching us, intrigued by her giddiness.

"Follow me," she said, darting into a stairwell. "Down here." She waited on the next landing in front of a fire escape door. "Don't worry, the alarm won't go off," she promised, flinging the door open onto a wide lawn surrounded by chestnut trees. "Drum roll, please," she announced. She snapped her fingers and half-jumped, half-flew through the open door. Just like that, my mother entered the outside world with its crashing skies and assorted other dangers.

"Agoraphobia isn't a fatal disease," she said. She kicked at some leaves, then bent down and picked up a shrivelled chestnut, lifted it to her nose and inhaled. "This is my special place, where I come to think and plan."

I stepped across the threshold gingerly, as if I were the one with the problem. The nausea had returned. My right eyelid started to twitch.

"Does this mean you'll be coming home?" I asked, picturing her standing out on the front lawn, sniffing fallen crabapples and waving to the neighbours. Despite the sunshine, the day was cold. She wrapped her arms around her shoulders and stepped out from under a tree.

"Home is still a problem," she said, coming a little closer and stretching an arm out toward me. "I know how hard this has been on you. What worries me is the responsibilities: the dirty dishes, the sticky floors, the wrinkled shirts, the unmade meals, the smudged windows. I'm worried about your father's heart, about Lissy. I'm worried about the Texaco, about pleasing Grammie, about having the right answers." Her face was getting darker. "And I'm worried about you," she said, "that you might stay angry with me forever."

Mom had hardly looked at me when I was at my angriest. Now it seemed that anger was the final brick in her bungalow of worry. Dad and Grammie were always accusing me of being mean-spirited, selfish and irresponsible. I usually thought they weren't being fair, but I felt guilty anyway. After all, hadn't I practically thrown my mother out the back door and tied her hands behind her back with a plan to toss her out the front door as well? Wasn't my anger what brought the whole house down?

"*Me* angry? Aren't you angry with me for what I made you do?"

"You were just trying to help," she said. "A part of me knew that even then."

Yes, if it hadn't been for me, Mom would never have done the impossible and locked herself inside the crawl space. But I didn't physically put her there. I would never have gone that far. My anger was never really at her, but her fears had poisoned the atmosphere in the house, made Lissy run away, sent Grammie to Europe, caused Dad to hide out in the bush with the crazy idea of starting a whole new life. And though I desperately wanted out, he put me in charge. So did Grammie. I didn't really have a choice.

"I wish we could start again. Maybe plan a trip to Montreal," she said, in that singsong voice I hated. Was it medication that allowed her to be outside amongst the chestnut trees today?

"I wish I could go to the Brown Derby with Ruby and the Arcadian Court with Ronnie and talk about nothing, girl talk, no need to explain." She reached out for me again. "I wish you could forgive me," she said.

I didn't say anything. I couldn't. Did forgiveness mean acceptance? We both headed for the door and ended up awkwardly squeezing through it together.

★

The family met with a judge to decide on custody of Lissy. Dad broke down. I could hardly bear to look at him. Men rarely cried, even on the soaps. Grammie was wearing her favourite bulldog face. No way she was breaking down. I felt increasingly unsettled. After my father's confessions (heart attack, overwork, loneliness, etc.) and Miss Clairy's advice (that everything stay the same for now), the judge, a guy at least as old as Grammie, cleared his throat.

"At this particular moment," he explained, "Mr. Tedley is not the best caregiver for his mentally retarded daughter. I believe everyone would agree with that assessment, Mr. Tedley included. And as for Mrs. Tedley," he continued, "Dr. McCurl, her psychiatrist, has expressed grave doubts as to whether she will be capable of resuming such a hefty responsibility, at least in the short run."

I thought about speaking up and telling him that Lissy could climb trees and outsmart adults, could run faster than anyone I knew. The way he was putting it, it sounded like Lissy was in a wheelchair unable to hold her neck up straight, eyeballs rolling around in her head.

"As long as Mrs. Tedley remains an in-patient at the Queen Street Mental Hospital, I can't help but see the family situation as precarious."

Grammie had been waiting her turn to speak. "Excuse me," she said. "Doesn't a grandmother count for anything in your books?"

Miss Clairy started to explain that Grammie had been travelling in Europe and didn't actually live at 6 Arizona Avenue, but Grammie interrupted with a condensed version of her own life, including how she'd saved her husband many years ago when he'd choked on an apple slice. Then she started talking about her love for Lissy.

"Now who do you think taught her her ABCs? She can still go all the way up to L without any help at all. I am indeed living at 6 Arizona Avenue now that I'm back in Canada. Don't even try telling me that a grandmother isn't preferable to a foster parent. None of this would have happened if I'd been at home." She paused long enough to give the judge a good dose of her see-all, know-all look. "Listen here, it's no wonder my son-in-law worries about being a good father. What decent man thinks that raising a mentally retarded child is a breeze? And as for my daughter, don't you think that worry over Melissa's well-being interferes with her own recovery?"

The judge frowned. "I understand what you're trying to say, but until five minutes ago, I didn't know you existed."

"Well, here I am, Lillian Gorman in the flesh," Grammie said. Was it possible that she was flirting with the judge? He couldn't seem to take his eyes off her. He glanced at my father and me, but didn't appear to find anything the least bit interesting about us. He turned his whole attention back to Grammie and delivered his summation to her.

"I'm going to suggest that we return Melissa Tedley to Arizona Avenue on a trial basis, as long as Lillian Gorman resides there and is in agreement with sending Melissa to a twenty-hour-a-week sheltered workshop and keeping in close touch with Miss Clairy, including weekly home visits. I hope I don't see you in my chambers again."

"We'd like her home by Christmas," said Grammie, chin in the air.

*

Dad and Mom and I sat politely in 999's not-so-sunny sun porch, rain pelting down on the hospital lawn. All Dad could talk about was the Texaco, the faulty gas pump, the busted peanut machine. I wished we were sitting outside under one of the chestnuts, inviting a lightning strike. Mom nodded, doing her best to pretend that gasoline was the most fascinating subject in the world.

I was feeling sick again. My stomach got queasy so often now that I was trying to figure out little things I could do to manage it.

I took a deep breath.

What if all the damn Texaco problems caused Mom to relapse? Was there something about my father that made everyone want to leave home? *Shut up,* I wanted to say, *shut the fuck up,* but I sealed my lips tight so I wouldn't accidentally speak. The TV in the far corner was tuned to Vietnam newscasts, the sound turned down. A woman with long grey hair was furiously biting her nails. A girl not much older than me was chewing gum so rapidly that her whole head vibrated. Finally, in the middle of Dad's description of how Queen Mary woke him up in the middle of the night puking up a fur ball, I blurted, "Mom, what do you do for fun around here?"

"Fun?" Mom asked, almost leaping on the word. "Well, there's occupational therapy. Things like macramé and découpage. Then there's the Games Room."

Acting half my age, struggling to control the tightness in my stomach, I begged for a game of anything. I dragged Mom to her feet, knowing Dad would follow.

In the Games Room, two male patients were playing checkers at a low table by the window. A woman was sitting by herself across from them, working on a jigsaw puzzle of the Grand Canyon. The walls were turquoise, and the room felt like it could be in the middle of the Caribbean. There was a Ping-Pong table. I pushed Dad to one end and handed him a paddle, then pulled Mom to the other end, a matching paddle clutched in her fist. "Come on," I encouraged, tossing the ball at Dad. He was standing there examining his paddle. The ball bounced off him and rolled toward Mom.

For a while they tapped the ball back and forth, click, click, click, click. Then Dad made a weak swipe, and Mom reacted quickly, smacking the ball smartly to the edge of the table on Dad's side and off.

"One nothing," I announced, which set Dad's blood boiling.

I refereed four games, two and two. Dad got so carried away toward the end that after a successful smash he cried out, "I was born for this game." Mom cheered her every point. Was keeping my parents entertained and sane such a difficult job? What if I quit school and dedicated my days to creating diversions like this. I'd have to wag my finger at Mom every so often, and remind her: "No more crawl spaces." I could fine Dad a dollar every time he let himself slump into a bad mood. There'd be no time to even think about my own life. Would that be good or bad?

By the time the visit was over, I was exhausted. Dad kissed Mom and patted her on the hip. She hugged me sideways. It wasn't until Dad and I were crossing the parking lot that he produced the Ping-Pong ball he'd taken as a souvenir, tossing it into the air and catching it with the other hand.

ELEVEN

ONE MORNING, LOOKING out the living room window the way my mother used to, I saw Diana Costello marching off bright and early to what Grammie later found out was a brand new job as a receptionist in a real estate office. She strutted by our house with a "We-don't-stop-for-nobody" look on her face, a brown paper bag lunch swinging from her right hand. The thought of any Costello doing something normal gave me hope. On Tuesday, a man and woman around my parents' ages moved into the empty Milford house. On Wednesday, Mr. Burr arrested a bank robber at Shopper's World mall. His picture was on the front page of both the *Telegram* and the *Star*.

Queen Mary caused a stir on Thursday, dragging home a stunned black squirrel that Grammie tried to feed a bit of toast to before setting it free. I'm not sure if the events were related, but Grammie gave up her apartment the same day. To top it all off, Mom was given a pass to spend Christmas at Arizona Avenue.

On my way to bed that night, I thought I heard Dad talking to himself in the dark kitchen. "We'll have a real tree this year," he was saying, "and we'll decorate it with popcorn and tinsel."

He was on the phone, talking nonsense to Mom.

"And on Christmas Eve, we'll go for a long walk in the snow, just the two of us. Then later you can hang one of your silk stockings over the edge of the bed. I want you, Flo. I want you so bad I could bite right through my tongue."

I wasn't proud of myself for listening in to that icky kind of talk, but I hoped it was what Mom wanted to hear. And I couldn't keep the same old fear from rising, the conviction that there would never be anything in our future that would ever equal the past.

*

Wendy and I were spending time together, though I wasn't sure yet what we were to one another. One afternoon in early December, we were standing at the top of her street with snowflakes melting on our lips.

"What do you think the future holds?" she asked. At first, I thought she was asking what chance my family might have at solving our problems. I didn't feel all that sure about anything. "For us," she added.

I stammered a little. "I feel better about…about you than… than about anyone or anything else."

She took a step closer. Her breath smelled like cold red licorice.

"Let's not worry," I said, though I was. Worrying that we'd end up exactly like my parents.

"Worry?"

In Wendy's world, worries knew their place and everything was frequently fine.

"What I mean," I explained, "is that being with you right here and now makes me happy."

She stepped onto the tops of my boots the way I used to dance with my Mom when I was a little kid, but there was nothing kid-like about what she did next. She wrapped her arms around my neck and pulled my mouth to hers. Then I had a new question to answer: could a boner poke a hole through several layers of winter clothes?

Aunt Veronica and Uncle Maurice were visiting Mom when we arrived at Queen Street the next day. They'd brought a box of chocolate-covered maraschino cherries and a Christmas cactus wrapped in red foil. They wore such big smiles I could see the tops of their gums.

"So, how is everyone?" Aunt Veronica asked, busying herself with fresh lipstick.

Dad made a croaking sound and commenced explaining how much he dreaded winter, all those cars needing a tow, all those dead batteries. Mom shut him up by pinching him on the knee. She had a complaint of her own.

"I'm feeling a little out of sorts. All people do here is blah-blah-blah about themselves."

Aunt Veronica stretched her hands out along the arms of her chair and wiggled her wrists, watching the light sparkle off the diamond on her finger. Uncle Maurice had that "Vote-for-Me" twinkle that he gave everyone, waitresses, neighbours, even total strangers on the street. Dad made the frog noise again and stared up at the ceiling.

"Enough about us," Mom said. "What's new with you?"

"I finally got a chance to wear that new red velvet dress to the Palais Royale last Saturday night," Aunt Veronica trilled. "You know the one with two crinolines? You should have seen me spinning across the floor."

"Not with me, of course," Uncle Maurice piped up. "Once I've had two glasses of champagne, I can't trust one foot to follow the other."

"I danced with the Deputy Mayor, three songs in a row," Aunt Veronica bragged. "My feet were a mess the next morning."

"But that didn't stop her," Uncle Maurice said. "We were off to the Variety Village Board brunch before noon on Sunday."

"I hobbled into the room," Aunt Veronica said, beaming. "Thank heavens I'd worn my New Mexico turquoise beads and that tight white silk shell."

"No one was looking at her feet."

By this time they were both whooping with laughter. Dad had a stunned look on his face, his mouth wide open. Mom looked like she'd been tapped by a magic wand and couldn't tell whether she was under a good spell or a bad one.

"Will there be a Christmas party here?" Aunt Veronica asked.

"Here?" Mom echoed.

"Yes. A party for the patients and staff. I could lend you that silver cocktail dress I wore to the Mayor's New Year's Levee last year. You'd look a perfect doll."

Dad perked up. "Are spouses invited?"

"It's not real, Ed. They don't have parties here."

"Well, I could talk to Dr. Sax's wife. She's on the hospital Board," said Aunt Veronica. "Maybe we could make it real."

Mom's face had drained of colour. She had that run-and-hide look in her eyes.

"I'd rather concentrate on coming home for Christmas this year," she said. "Let's hold off on the silver dress for now."

The silence made breathing difficult, but then Aunt Veronica plunged back into happy mode and we all sat together, trying our best to smile.

★

I'd aced a week of exams, proving how much information I had packed into my brain. For example, $a + b = b + a$, no matter what. I knew that graphite mixed with clay made pencil lead. I knew that August 6th, 1945 was the day America dropped an atomic bomb on Hiroshima. But I still didn't have a clue where fear came from, whether it was a lethal mixture of bad experiences or something built right into a person. I didn't know why I couldn't turn shattered nerves into nerves of steel. Retardation, heart trouble, agoraphobia, nausea, blizzards: why did they exist? Why was something always lurking in the shadows, ready to leap out and ruin everything?

The week before Christmas, I tackled Lissy's neglected room. I dusted her entire collection of knick-knacks and stuffed animals. I lugged Christmas decorations up from the basement, hung mistletoe over every doorframe, wrapped a gold and silver garland around the dining room chandelier. I strung coloured lights in the lower branches of the crabapple tree.

Grammie and I scurried off to Shopper's World to do our Christmas shopping. The crowds were terrible. I wanted to buy Lissy a bike, but the prices were too high. All I had was forty dollars. Instead, I settled for a pair of roller skates on sale. For Aunt Ruby and Uncle Frank, I bought a book of off-colour jokes called *Love Begins at 50* and a big bottle of bubble bath. For Aunt Veronica and Uncle Maurice, I found matching His and Her hand towels decorated with little blue crowns. I even found a red imitation-leather autograph book for Roma that she would probably fill with the signatures of Toronto aldermen.

I bought Wendy a claddagh ring—a crowned heart held by two hands. A Canadian Football board game for Marco, who was seriously depressed now that the season was over. And when Grammie wasn't looking, I bought her a *FOODS OF THE WORLD* apron, with little pictures of steaming platters of spaghetti, tacos, wiener schnitzel, fish and chips and egg rolls.

I spotted a pair of black satiny ballerina-like slippers for Mom. *Dancer's Desire*, they were called, "guaranteed to make you feel you are dancing on air." They were the perfect indoor shoes for her. Dad was more difficult. I could hear him complaining about everything. "Too pricey, too gimmicky, too useless." I had given up and was headed for the tie rack in Eaton's when I noticed a T-shirt store promising appliquéd personal messages.

ED TEDLEY, the finished shirt read, *TEXACO KING*.

Later that day, Grammie sent me up to Kingston Road where the fruit market was selling Christmas trees, and I bought a real Scotch pine about six feet tall. As I dragged it back to the house through powdery snow, the fragrance went right to my head.

Christmas was going to be fine, I'd make sure of it. I was still fighting the queasiness, but the more deeply I inhaled the better I could control it.

Before dinner I hauled Dad into the living room where the Christmas tree stood bare. "You take the left and I'll take the right," I ordered, handing him a string of lights. We worked slowly. The frosted glass ornaments, dangling on loops of thread, threw coloured light around the room. A tiny wooden manger fit perfectly on a bottom branch, as if it had grown there, out in the forest.

Dad held the angel in his hands, his arms half-raised. "And now for the final touch," he said with a flourish. In the shimmer of red, green and yellow light, the angel's long fine hair was platinum. "She looks like your mother," he said.

After a year packed away in a cardboard box, I thought, but refrained from saying it. I didn't want to knock the dazzle from his eyes.

*

On Christmas Eve, Grammie and I were waiting at the living room window, watching as the Burr family piled bags of presents into the trunk of their car and drove off, leaving Barfy howling in the empty house. Every front yard except for the Remingtons' was lit up. Arizona Avenue was all winter rainbows.

Lissy was the first of our Christmas gifts to arrive. She practically fell out of Miss Clairy's car, her arms and legs going in so many directions she seemed to be spinning. She barged through the front door and threw her arms around Grammie.

"Don't hesitate to call if there's a problem," Miss Clairy said.

Lissy pawed me, cooing like a huge pigeon.

"She's happy," Grammie said, her glasses knocked crooked, her steel-wool hair a mess.

By the time we had calmed Lissy down and she was poking amongst the brightly wrapped presents, we heard Dad's Valiant crunch to a stop in the driveway. Grammie looked at me and

I looked at her. All the clocks in the house seemed to stop. Even the Christmas tree was holding its breath. My heart was hanging above an invisible trampoline. Santa Claus, the Easter Bunny, the Tooth Fairy: none of these creatures had ever seemed as unreal as Mom did that Christmas Eve.

"She's home," Grammie said solemnly, which sounded as far-fetched to me as "The moon is made of cheese."

But reality happens, for better or worse. Cold and ruddy-looking, as if she'd travelled from the North Pole, Mom's face appeared in the front hall. The rest of her followed, including the bag of foil-wrapped gifts that was swinging from one of her arms. She dropped the bag then stepped back out onto the porch. Lissy stared at the front hall, her smile spooky. Dad entered the house with a stomp, flicking the snow from his moustache with a flourish. "Just give her a second to catch her breath," he said. Was she leaning against the front porch railing, repeating over and over that this was it, there was nowhere else to go?

I counted all the way up to forty-two before she reappeared, looking perfectly calm. She walked into the hall and unbuttoned her coat. She stole a few glances at the ceiling. She seemed pleased that the living room curtains were wide open and that the Christmas tree cast such a big reflection in the window that it seemed to be both inside and outside at once. We sat down around the tree and Mom emptied her bag of gifts, carefully spreading them in amongst the ones already beneath the tree. She sank into her favourite chair and Lissy curled up at her feet, laying her head in Mom's lap, humming a tune made up of three notes. For once Dad didn't complain that the sound was driving him crazy.

*

On Christmas morning everything was strangely calm. In Vietnam, there was a ceasefire. Same in Ireland, where Protestants and Catholics were strolling the streets together. Grammie sat on the couch looking grandmotherly while Lissy leaned against her, roller skates on the wrong feet, stuffed animals piled in her lap. Mom was beautiful in her new black ballet slippers. Dad was wearing his *TEXACO KING* T-shirt with his old saggy pajama bottoms. He looked like the kind of dad who could be King, at least for a day.

And then there were my presents: a tie-dyed tank top, a pair of psychedelic purple cords, the new Monkees' album, an Alfred E. Newman calendar, a whoopee cushion, several *Man from U.N.C.L.E.* pocketbooks and a white shirt with a Nehru collar. I spent the late morning and early afternoon playing a homemade game on the living room rug with Lissy: each of her stuffed animals were whisked away on a roller skate to the Planet Whoopee Cushion. The smell of roasting turkey got stronger and stronger. The uncles and aunts arrived at dinnertime, with another round of presents. Aunt Veronica and Uncle Maurice loved their His and Her hand towels so much they tucked them into their collars like fancy bibs. Roma asked each of us to sign our names in her autograph book. And Aunt Ruby and Uncle Frank kept us all in stitches with *Love Begins at 50* dirty jokes, mainly about breasts and farts.

By ten o'clock, Aunt Veronica, Uncle Maurice and Roma were gone. The sky was full of stars. Aunt Ruby and Uncle Frank were singing a Christmas medley while doing the dishes. Lissy was curled up fast asleep under the tree, the last unopened present in Scarborough. Grammie was beaming, still wearing the red paper hat from her Christmas cracker. Mom and Dad sat together on the couch, holding hands.

*

I slipped out of the house early on Boxing Day, before Mom went back to 999. Christmas Day already felt like a dream. When the frosty morning-after air hit me, it hurt at first to breathe.

I was on my way to Marco's house to give him his present, wondering on the way whether Christmas was a new beginning or just a big show to cover up all the bad feelings and fears? I was worrying again. It seemed entirely likely that as soon as I had left the house, Mom and Dad would fall back into their old habits.

Mrs. Morelli invited me into her plastic living room. Marco liked his game of Canadian Football as much as I liked my James Bond jigsaw puzzle. We played a few rounds of football and Mrs. Morelli served us Brio and almond cookies. By the time I got home, Mom was gone. I hadn't wanted to stick around for the goodbyes, didn't want to pretend that going back to a mental hospital was a normal thing to do on Boxing Day. The presence of the mother who had spent weeks in bed and ended up almost dying in the crawl space beneath the back porch was still in every corner of the house. The Christmas mother that had breezed in two nights ago had to be an hallucination. Watching her go would have been like staring into thin air.

★

In the middle of a knockdown blizzard, I gave Wendy the ring. We met halfway between our houses, at the laundromat, a few blocks east of the Texaco. The front windows were so steamy no one could see in and we couldn't see out. With the washers whooshing and the driers clattering, we exchanged gifts. I ripped into mine, a knitted purple scarf. She undid hers more slowly, carefully lifting the lid off the box.

"Oh my God," she exclaimed, twirling it around her finger. It was at least one size too big.

"I can exchange it."

"No way!" She held the ring away from me. "I'll put tape around it until my fingers grow." She held the ring out at arm's length and waved it up and down in the air.

We sat on a bench and as we talked about going steady, about the upcoming Valentine's dance, about Valhalla Park and how beautiful it would be again in the spring, I surrendered to the laundromat's heat and Wendy's soft voice. She even mentioned my birthday, January 17th, hinting at what she might get me. "I love to plan ahead," she said.

I stayed two hours with Wendy. By the time I arrived home, the blizzard had turned Arizona Avenue into an anywhere, anonymous. Each house was exactly the same as the one next to it, and the sameness made the street appear incredibly small. The Costellos' bungalow had not a trace of drunkenness to it. Except for the lack of Christmas lights, you'd never have a clue that the Remingtons were Jehovah's Witnesses. Lonny Milford's place was nothing but a roof, some walls and lots and lots of snow. In the Burrs' front yard, Barfy had yet to leave a single print.

*

When the world grows old, I'll probably still remember the blue plaid jacket I wore to Aunt Ruby and Uncle Frank's New Year's Eve party and the hors d'oeuvres I ate and the four glasses of champagne I sampled. I won't soon forget the five-foot snowbanks lining the streets or the whooping, clanging, screeching sounds of midnight as heard from Aunt Ruby and Uncle Frank's apartment balcony. I'll even remember what the first of 1967 felt like. But most of all, I'll never forget the few minutes before we left for the party.

Grammie was in the bathroom, trying, she said, to take years off her face, and Dad, in his underpants, was sitting on the edge of the bed, in a good mood, whistling an old song and shining his shoes. Mom, on another two-day pass from the hospital, sat on the orange chair in the living room, looking out the window. She was wearing the black ballet slippers I'd given her. Her platinum blonde hair shone like cream against the black of her party dress. The room still smelled of Christmas, the sound of my father's whistling was gentle and dreamy.

"Would you like to dance?" she asked, turning toward me.

"Dance?"

"I read somewhere that Princess Grace likes to dance with her son the Prince."

Was this what normal mothers and sons did together? Nothing

183

normal about princes and princesses. "What would we dance to?" I asked.

She smiled and nodded toward the music of Dad's whistling. I wasn't sure how to fit myself into her arms, or whether it was she who should fit into me. We bumped elbows and I stepped on the toe of her right slipper, but somehow we began to manage. At first, there was no rhythm. She was intent on moving one way, me another. Her hand felt strangely small in mine. It wouldn't be long before I'd outgrow her; I was already up to her eyebrows. I stepped on her toes a half a dozen more times, until we finally settled into a kind of sway. It felt like the house was rocking a little. The sky could topple, LBJ could win the Vietnam War, "Winchester Cathedral" could replace "God Save the Queen" as the galaxy's most popular song. Mom was looking into my eyes. I wasn't entirely convinced that the bad times were really over, but I felt no need to worry right then. We continued to move together even after Dad stopped whistling and started muttering, grumbling again. A more usual kind of music.

★   ★   ★

ACKNOWLEDGEMENTS

I tell my creative writing students that a poem is an Olympic dive—one toe out of line and the whole thing can be ruined. A short story is a hundred-metre dash, precision and pacing inseparable. A novel is a longer challenge, like swimming the English Channel. You start off with perfect strokes, developing stamina, making sure to measure out your energy bit by bit. But by the time land is in sight, you're clawing at the water, panting, even panicking, doing whatever is necessary not to drown.

Thanks to Glenn Hayes, Pat Jasper and Sharon Wilston for getting themselves wet early on in the process and helping to steer me in the right direction.

I am eternally grateful to Brian Vanderlip for walking on water every now and again.

What good fortune it was when Alayna Munce drew up alongside me with her boatful of maps, nourishment and inspirational advice. She never once suggested that my turning blue was anything other than a temporary chill.

I am also deeply indebted to my publisher Beth Follett for diving in at a crucial moment and reminding me of the miracles that grace and resilience can produce. She is one hell of a good swimmer! Thanks to Zab Hobart for making such a beautiful book.

I am most beholden to my wife, Karen Dempster, who never left my side from the first day I dipped my toe into the water to that final lunge for dry land. I swear that she was often moving ahead of me, making a path between the waves.

Finally, many thanks to friends and readers who have been waiting on the far shore in all kinds of weather for the book and me to arrive.

BARRY DEMPSTER is an award-winning poet, author, editor and mentor. He lives in Holland Landing, Ontario.